HOLLY & THE RUINED PARTY

The Holly Lewis Mystery Series - Book 6

BY

DIANNE HARMAN

Published by: Dianne Harman
www.dianneharman.com

Interior, cover design and website by
Vivek Rajan

ISBN: 9781659629927

CONTENTS

ACKNOWLEDGMENTS

Hosting a party can make even the calmest person a bit nervous. I know, because for several years when my husband was a California State Senator, I hosted parties at least weekly, sometimes more. And trust me, things went wrong!

Ever spilled the main course minutes before the first guest is to arrive? That's when I was forced to invoke the "Julia Child five second rule" – it's permissible to pick food up off the floor if it's been there less than five seconds!

I never had the courage to host a party when I was Holly's age, so I decided to write this book from a young woman's perspective of hosting a party when a lot of things go wrong!

To Holly and everyone else who has the courage to host parties, I admire you!

To all of the dedicated people who help my stories come alive, thank you!

And to Tom, my biggest fan and harshest critic, thank you!

Win FREE Paperbacks every week!

Go to www.dianneharman.com/freepaperback.html and get your FREE copies of Dianne's books and favorite recipes immediately by signing up for her newsletter.

Once you've signed up for her newsletter you're eligible to win three paperbacks. One lucky winner is picked every week. Hurry before the offer ends!

PROLOGUE

It was a cool fall night in Cottonwood Springs. The trees had begun to turn and there were leaves scratching along the pavement as a breeze picked up and sent them scuttling along the street. A few sparse clouds floating across the night sky, illuminated by an almost full moon.

There had been a cold snap a little over a week ago, but now it had warmed up a bit. The evenings were still cool, but during the day it had been fairly nice, which seemed to work in their favor, because this would have been much harder to do if there had been an early snow. This time of year in Colorado that was always a possibility.

They'd tried everything they could think of to stop the surprise party Holly Lewis was giving for Fiona Garcia. Sabotaging it the best way they knew how and still, she wasn't deterred. They had to try one last time to derail this party. One last ditch effort to sink it once and for all. They couldn't give up. Not yet. The party had to be stopped. Their pride depended on it.

Their first attempt to stop the party only took a few phone calls. Cottonwood Springs wasn't a big town, so there were only so many places where you could order a cake or food. They'd called and canceled the orders for the party, thinking that would deter her from having the party. They were hoping someone that was Holly's age wouldn't think to double-check and make sure it was all in order. But apparently, she had, because the party was still scheduled as planned.

That meant they had to get a little more creative. But that was easier said than done. After all, they didn't want anyone to know they were the one who had caused the party to be ruined. But they were definitely going to have to use a more extreme approach in order to achieve their goal, which was why they were prowling around so late at night, hoping to use the cover of darkness in order to keep their identity a secret.

It hadn't been easy to get a copy of the key to the recreation room for the church, but they had. It was a good thing Missy had made copies of the key that were hanging in her office. The fact that Missy rarely, if ever, locked it made it even easier. Now all they needed to do was sneak in without being spotted. That's why they waited until late at night to make one final attempt to ensure that the party Holly was throwing for her aunt Fiona was a failure.

They'd known better than to park in the church parking lot and instead parked one block away. All the lights were out in the nearby houses, so it didn't seem likely that anyone would notice. It had been nerve-wracking to walk down the alley, hoping there weren't any dogs they might startle and cause them to bark. But, thank goodness, there hadn't been. The only creature they'd found in the alley was a stray cat out hunting. It had pounced on a leaf tumbling by, thinking that it was something tasty before going on about its business. Hardly anyone would be out on foot at this time of year.

Staying in the shadows, they crept up to the recreation room door at the back of the church. They heard a car on the street, so they ducked back into the safety of the shadows until the headlights had passed by. Granted, the person in the car probably wouldn't think anything was going on, but they didn't want to take the chance.

They recognized the car and knew the people who owned it were good at figuring things out, so they didn't feel they should push their luck. Better not to be seen, just in case Holly decided to look for whoever had destroyed her party plans. When the car was gone, they hurried to slide the key into the keyhole and turn the deadbolt.

Within seconds, they were in the room.

They let the door close softly behind them and considered turning on the lights, but decided against it. There was no need to let people passing by know that someone was in the building. Lights would almost certainly attract attention at this time of night.

Most of the people in Cottonwood Springs were asleep with the exception of those people who worked the night shift at a couple of the local factories. But those people were at work, not decorating a recreation room. The sheriff was good at his job, so if he happened by and noticed, he'd almost certainly stop and check to see why there were lights on and verify that everything was okay. And it wouldn't be. They'd be caught in the act, and they couldn't let that happen.

Instead, they went to the row of windows and twisted the control rod on the blinds so they were partially open. The glow from the street lights outside lit up the room well enough they could see once they allowed their eyes to adjust to the semi-darkness. It was easy to make out the streamers, the banner and all the other decorations. The room certainly seemed festive enough for a great party. Too bad they were going to have to wreck the whole thing.

It was obvious Holly had put a lot of time and effort into decorating the room, not to mention money. But they had a goal, and it wasn't going to get accomplished unless they trashed everything in sight.

They walked slowly over to the nearest table, surveying the centerpiece that looked like a fashion model standing among the glittery tinsel strands. She was cartoon-like, but still a nice addition to the table considering the party was to celebrate Fiona's debut in the fashion industry.

Pieces of confetti that said things like "Wow!" "Way to go!" and "Amazing!" were strewn all over the tables. There were even papers in the center for guests to write their best wishes or sentiments on, so that Fiona could read them later. Balloon bouquets were in the corners and streamers of different colors ran back and forth across the ceiling.

Benches were on two sides of the room with brightly colored pillows on them. There were more decorations on another nearby table, but they'd seen enough. It wasn't like they were there to enjoy the decorations. They were there to destroy them.

They reached their hand out slowly towards a centerpiece and knocked it over. It made a satisfying thump as it toppled over onto the table. Smiling to themselves, they picked up the sheets of paper and tossed them in the air. Each sheet fluttered down to the floor, scattering all around them.

Starting off slowly, they destroyed the decorations on the table before finally jerking the tablecloth completely off. It tumbled to the floor before they released their grip on it, letting it fall down.

As they moved to the next table, they reached up and tugged on the streamers, giggling a little when they felt them start to tear. They felt a little guilty for what they were doing, but who hadn't ever wanted to wreck a room that looked like this? Secretly they'd always wanted to do something like this and now was their chance. If they were going to do it, then they were going to enjoy doing it.

As they tugged on the next group of streamers, the tape broke free from the ceiling and made a small popping noise. Really getting into the destruction they were causing, they did a little pirouette which caused the torn streamers to flutter around them.

Before long, they were mindlessly tearing things down, knocking tables over, and popping the balloons. They shredded the streamers as they pulled them down, tossed other things on the floor, and did their best to wreck absolutely everything they touched.

By the time they were finished, it looked as though a herd of buffalo had trampled through the room, destroying everything in it. They hadn't left a single decoration untouched. When it was all done, they stopped and surveyed the damage.

Chest heaving from the excitement, the reality of their actions set in. There was a flash of remorse, but what was done couldn't be undone, not that they would have anyway. They'd wanted to do this, even if they did feel a little bad about it.

"That should be good," they said aloud to themselves. "Let's see her bounce back after finding out about this. There's no way she can continue with the party when she finds out that everything's been destroyed. She'll have no choice but to cancel it."

As they looked over the room, enjoying their handiwork, they spotted the door that led to the little kitchen. Most of the people who used the room kept snacks or spare items back there. Crossing the room, they decided they better do a quick check to make sure there wasn't anything in there that needed to be destroyed.

Decorations could be replaced, but if they'd left something in the kitchen, the party could still be salvaged. In order to make sure this didn't happen, they had to be as thorough as possible.

They pushed the swinging door open and turned on the lights. With no outside windows in the kitchen, there was no way anyone would spot them in there. It was completely enclosed, without even a window facing the rec room.

There was nothing on the counter but plates, plasticware, cups, and napkins. They almost passed by them, but then remembered that they were setting out to completely destroy the party. Leaving anything salvageable would not accomplish their goal. They turned around and began pulling the items out of the protective plastic wrap and tossed them around the room.

Everything flew up in the air and landed on the ground, making them unusable. The plastic utensils clattered to the ground right before the plates fell down. Lastly, the napkins fluttered around them and down to the ground.

Tiptoeing over the items on the floor on their way to the refrigerator, they pulled it open and found finger sandwiches laid out on platters. There were also deli cheeses and meats arranged neatly on others.

They were a little disappointed that there was no cake, but they had to satisfy themselves with what was on hand, although ruining a cake would have been very satisfying. Unfortunately, there was no way they could break into the bakery and destroy it. They'd have to be satisfied with just ruining the snacks.

They pulled off the plastic domes on the trays. Pausing for a moment to look at the sandwiches, they picked one up and popped it in their mouth before tossing the rest of them in the air. With a sudden jerk, they flipped the first platter so that the food would go flying out all at once. Each one flew apart, causing every layer to separately hit the floor with a plop. They did the same with the rest of the platters. Taking each one out, they removed the plastic cover before they tossed it all on the floor.

"Don't think there's going to be a party now," they said smugly. "There's no way she can replace all of this in such a short time. Grinning, they walked out of the kitchen, flipping the light switch off as they left.

Walking confidently across the room, they double-checked that they hadn't missed anything. Satisfied they'd done enough damage, they put their hand on the door and pushed it open. Their only regret was they wouldn't be here to see the shocked look on Holly's face when she realized that her party was destroyed.

Stepping out into the cool night air, they gently closed the door behind them and locked it. They'd have to satisfy themselves with what they imagined the reaction would be. Probably shock and then frustration. But there would be no reason to suspect them. It was a flawless plan. They were confident there was no way they could be caught.

CHAPTER ONE

Enjoying the fall weather, Brigid, Linc, and Holly had spent an afternoon together enjoying just being together as a family. They'd gone to the store, rented a movie, and then come home to cook dinner together.

They were making popcorn before they watched the movie when Linc remembered that no one had cleaned the room that their last guest had been in after he'd checked out.

Linc couldn't stand to let it wait, and he promised he'd be back in just a few minutes as he'd hurried next door to their B & B to take care of it. Brigid told him she'd finish up the popcorn and that she and Holly would wait for him to return before they started watching the movie.

Holly didn't mind waiting since it gave her some extra time to think about the party she was planning to give for her aunt, Fiona. It had been a big deal for Fiona to have a major clothing manufacturer buy her designs, and Holly felt it was important for people to acknowledge and celebrate her success.

Fiona didn't like people to make a big deal over her, preferring to stay behind the scenes and celebrate others' accomplishments. But Holly and Brigid both felt this was big enough that Fiona deserved some recognition for her achievement. It was bad enough Fiona wasn't even telling people about it, and Holly was determined to make sure everyone knew.

"Do you think it's weird I'm excited to throw this party?" Holly asked Brigid as they were sitting on the couch in the great room. They had the movie they'd rented in the player, and they were waiting for Linc to come back from next door. It had been quite a while since the three of them had sat down for a movie night.

Holly was a little surprised at how much she was looking forward to something so simple. Jett was on the floor by Brigid's feet while Holly's dog, Lucky, was curled up beside her on the couch.

"Not at all," Brigid said with a smile. "And you should be. If you think about it, you're partly responsible for Fiona making it this far." Brigid's red hair was down and flowing around her shoulders. It seemed to have grown so much lately, and Holly was glad she hadn't cut it yet. The longer look was good on her even though Brigid constantly threatened to chop it all off. Sometimes Holly was sure she said it just to get a reaction from her.

"Why do you think that?" Holly questioned. She didn't see how she could be at all responsible for Fiona and her success. After all, it was Fiona's talent that had gotten her this far.

"If you hadn't convinced her to put her designs online on that social media profile, that company never would have found her," Brigid pointed out. "She could sew and plan all day, but without that exposure, she'd still just be dreaming. With your nudge and encouragement, you sent her in the right direction."

"I guess I kind of did, huh?" Holly asked with a smile. She hadn't really thought about it that way. She'd just been encouraging Fiona to get out there and let others see how talented she was. There'd been no other thought beyond that.

Fiona's designs were so amazing Holly had felt people needed to see them. Keeping them a secret would have been the same as Leonardo da Vinci never sharing his work. What a tragedy that would have been. Holly was a firm believer that anything wonderful and artistic should be shared with the world so it could be properly appreciated.

But Holly knew that Brigid was right. Fiona would probably never have put her designs online without Holly's suggestions and encouragement. She'd just barely been convinced to give it a try for a little while when the company, Green Butterfly, sent her a direct message and wanted to talk with her. Everything changed with that one little message. Suddenly she was talking with people who could make her dreams come to life, and it all seemed to happen in the blink of an eye.

"You certainly helped her come out of her shell, I can tell you that," Brigid said proudly. "She listens to you in a way that she never did with me."

"I'm glad," Holly said, nodding. "Fiona deserves recognition for her creativity. But I'm not sure why you think she listens to me more, because I've seen where she's listened to you."

"Maybe it's just the big sister thing," Brigid sighed. "She was always determined to do the opposite of what I told her when we were younger."

"I can understand that," Holly chuckled. "But she doesn't do it to make you mad. She's just independent like that."

"That she is," Brigid agreed. "Which is probably one of the qualities that has brought her this far in the first place. But I think you should know that you deserve some of that praise. You did a good thing, and it's really made a difference in someone else's life. I'm very proud of you."

The look she gave Holly told her that Brigid was being sincere. She could tell by the way Brigid had raised her chin when she'd spoken that she really was proud.

Holly felt the prick of tears at her eyes as her nose began to burn.

"Thank you," she said. "That means a lot to me." Before Brigid came into her life, she didn't have a whole lot of people who would say things like that to her. So when it did happen, it still made her a little emotional.

"Anytime," Brigid said as she leaned over and squeezed Holly's hand. "Now if only Linc would hurry up so we can get the movie started. I swear, he's seriously obsessed with keeping things immaculate over at the B & B. I understand it to a certain extent, but people aren't going to care which throw pillow is in front of the other." She leaned back and sighed as she picked up her popcorn bowl and tossed a piece in her mouth.

"What do you think Fiona's going to do about the bookstore if this fashion line of hers takes off?" Holly asked. She'd been thinking about it recently, but hadn't had the nerve to bring it up before now. If anyone would have an idea what Fiona might do, it would be Brigid.

"I hadn't really thought about it," Brigid admitted. "But it could be an issue down the road. Especially if she has to make more designs or if they need her to fly wherever it is they do things. Have you asked her about it?"

"No," Holly admitted. "I didn't know quite how to approach the subject. It's not that I don't trust her to do the right thing, and she needs to keep her attention on the clothing design business, because it could really take her places. And if she decided to sell the store, who could blame her?"

Although when Holly thought about anyone else owning the bookstore, it made her stomach churn. What if the new owner changed everything that made the store so unique? Holly wasn't sure if she could stand to see that happen.

"Read It Again" was known for its eclectic feel, friendly staff, and coziness. Customers were encouraged to take their time when choosing books and there were even comfortable chairs scattered around the store for them to sit in and read through the first few chapters of a book.

Fiona also provided a coffeepot and mugs for anyone who wanted a cup of coffee. Who else would do that? Not many store owners, that was for sure. If someone else took over, they might end up killing the exact thing that had made the bookstore such an amazing place to begin with.

"Don't think about it for now," Brigid said as she waved her hand. "No need to worry about something that hasn't happened yet. Who's to say Fiona hasn't already thought of it? She's a smart woman and seems to be a natural in business. She's probably got a backup plan and then a backup plan for her backup plan," she teased. "Nothing gets past her. She's prepared for almost anything."

"She does always seem to know what she's doing, even when she's just winging it," Holly admitted. "You're probably right. I'll just sit back and enjoy the ride while it lasts." The more she thought about it, the more she realized that Fiona wouldn't sell to anyone who wanted to change the bookstore. If anything, she'd probably make sure that nothing was changed in her absence.

"That's the spirit," Brigid said happily. She pulled a blanket from the back of the couch and draped it across her legs. It brushed across the top of Jett's head and he looked up, curious. But a noise at the front door distracted him, and he turned to see what it was. Lucky took notice too, jumping up and letting out a little growl as the door opened.

"Sorry it took me so long," Linc said as he hurried in through the door. He surprised the dogs who both let out soft barks at the sudden noise, but then relaxed when they realized it wasn't an intruder. "I wanted to make sure everything was ready. You know how I am about keeping the rooms clean." He hurried into the kitchen as he spoke.

"No problem," Brigid said. "We were just talking while we waited for you." She smiled fondly as she looked over her shoulder at him.

"About what?" he asked as he washed his hands and then got a bowl of popcorn.

"Mainly Fiona's party," Holly supplied.

"Have you decided where you're going to have it?" he asked. "You're getting down to the wire here."

"I know," Holly admitted. "But I don't have a clue where to even start looking. I probably should have found it first." She knew there were rooms and halls that people rented in order to have parties and get-togethers, but she had no idea how to go about getting one of those room. It was the one thing she'd been putting off. It was past time for her to figure it out.

"Why don't you use the recreation room at the church?" Brigid asked with a snap of her fingers. It was as if the idea had never come to her until that very moment.

"Do they do that?" Holly asked. "I haven't ever noticed a rec room there." She knew the church was big and had a lot of rooms she'd never been in, but she thought she'd know if there was a recreation room.

"They do," Brigid nodded. "It's really nice, and I'm sure Missy would let you use it. She stopped advertising the room for rent because most people went with a smaller place. Now she kind of does it by word of mouth. But for your party and as many people that are probably going to show up, you need a bigger room."

"Awesome," Holly grinned. "I'll talk to Missy in the morning."

"And now that you have one less thing to worry about," Linc said, "are you ready for the movie?"

"Definitely," Holly said eagerly. "I've been waiting to see this one."

"You know it's been out for a while, right?" Linc paused. He looked at Holly as if he were concerned for her.

"Yeah, I know," she nodded. "But I don't ever seem to have time to sit and enjoy a full movie. I've been putting this one off until I could actually watch the whole thing."

Between school, work at the bookstore, and the occasional tutoring that she sometimes did, she didn't have much spare time. Throw in planning a party and helping Brigid and Linc maintain their website meant there was almost no time to sit down and watch a movie from start to finish.

"I hope it was worth the wait," Linc said as he settled in next to Brigid and pressed play on the remote control.

CHAPTER TWO

The next morning, Holly woke up with a smile on her face, ready to face the day. She planned on talking to Missy this morning about the recreation room, and she was hopeful it would be the last thing she needed to cross off her party list. Even if she needed to pay a little to reserve it, she was more than willing to as long as she had somewhere to hold the party.

She was planning to have the party that coming weekend, and she didn't want to have to postpone it. Cold weather was forecast, along with snow, so she didn't want to try to get people together when they'd rather stay in their warm homes. With any luck, this would be the final thing to get the ball rolling.

Stretching, she climbed out of bed and sighed. As long as everything went well today, she'd be able to feel a load lifted off her shoulders. Lucky stirred from his favorite spot on her bed, his little eyes slowly opening before he stretched and yawned.

"I've got a full day ahead of me, Lucky," she said as she scratched his head. "But hopefully, everything will go my way." She stood and stretched again before shuffling over to her closet and deciding what to wear.

Brigid and Linc had already gone over to the B & B to welcome their next guest, leaving her home alone, not that she minded. She loved Brigid and Linc with her whole heart, but that didn't mean she didn't enjoy a little quiet time, especially in the mornings.

After she was dressed, she walked into the great room and Lucky followed her. She looked at him, his little tail wagging in greeting, and said, "I have to go see Missy this morning." She stepped closer to him and scratched his cheeks. "I bet she'd like to see you. I don't know when the last time was she got to see how cute you've turned out to be."

Missy had helped Holly clean Lucky up when she'd first found him by the side of the road. His coat hadn't been nearly as shiny then, and he'd been much skinnier. Now he was healthy looking and handsome. "Why don't you come with me?" she said as she bent over and scooped him up. "I'm sure she won't mind."

For a moment, she considered going over to the B & B to tell Linc and Brigid where she was going, but decided not to bother them. She knew they were often busy in the morning and unless she was able to help, she didn't like to get in the way. Instead, she wrote them a note and then carried Lucky to her car.

"It's been a while since just the two of us were able to take a ride, huh?" she said to Lucky as she climbed behind the wheel of her Volkswagen Bug. Lucky seemed happy to be back in her car with her, riding around like they used to. Holly made a mental note that she needed to try to do it a little more regularly. As excited as he seemed to be, it was apparent the little guy had missed doing it.

As they drove through town, Lucky excitedly watched everything as it went by. He eagerly barked at passing cars and jumped up and down when he saw someone riding a bicycle. Holly giggled at his excitement, but was glad when they finally got to the church. His barks had grown louder and louder in the small car and her attempts to get him to quiet down were futile.

"Calm down," Holly said as he put his paws up on the passenger window and barked with excitement. "I don't want you to bark in here. You're going to give me a headache." She scooped him up before climbing out of her car.

When she stepped out of it, she saw leaves sliding noisily across the pavement as the wind picked up. Lucky squirmed in her hands, wanting to chase the leaves. She had to tighten her grip on his tiny, wiggling body so she wouldn't accidentally drop him.

"No," she said in a strong voice, and the dog became calm. She was grateful he understood that it was time to stop when she grew firm with him. "You can't chase leaves in town, Lucky. You'd have to watch for cars, and I know you won't. Come on, once we're inside, I'm sure Missy will enjoy giving you lots of love." Heading for the door, she pulled it open and stepped out of the wind.

As she entered the church through a side door, Holly knew where most of the doors led to, but it was a pretty big church, and there were more rooms in it than she'd ever had a chance to explore.

She walked to the room that she knew held all the spare food for the food pantry and turned to the door on the opposite side of the hall. Raising her hand, she knocked on the door. She knew this was Missy's office, but wasn't sure if she'd be in there. Missy was always so busy it was hard to say where she might be at any given time.

"Come in," Missy's voice called out pleasantly from inside. Lucky's ears perked at the sound, and Holly couldn't help but smile at his reaction. He obviously remembered her. Turning the doorknob, she entered the small office.

"Holly!" Missy cried out as she stood up. "I'm so glad to see you. It feels like it's been ages." She circled her desk and pulled her into a strong hug.

"I know," Holly said as she hugged her back. Lucky was still in her arms, attempting to lick Missy's face. "Everyone has been so busy, but I needed to talk to you, so Lucky and I decided to pay you a visit."

"I'm so glad you did," Missy said as she let Lucky give her kisses.

He leapt for her arms and they both laughed as Missy had to catch him in his eagerness. "Whoa there, Lucky. Just relax. Let's sit down," she said as she turned back to Holly. "Now tell me what I can do for you."

Missy carried Lucky around the desk to her seat, as Holly sat in one of the chairs in front of the desk. They were different than the ones she'd seen before. These looked new and were a beautiful shade of dark blue velvet-like material. Holly couldn't help but run her hands along them. They were soft and luxurious, and she kind of wished she had one for her bedroom.

"I don't know if you've heard, but Fiona is getting a big break with her clothing designs," Holly began. She knew Fiona hadn't told many people, but that didn't mean that word hadn't spread. Especially since Brigid and Missy spoke often.

"I heard something about it a while back from Brigid. I've been so busy I haven't been able to catch up to find out where things are now. Last I knew, she had a company who wanted to see some of her designs," Missy said as she played with Lucky who was sitting on her lap.

Holly nodded. "That's right. They loved them, and they're going to start producing them and handling the distribution. I want to have a celebration party for her, but I've run into a snag. I don't have anywhere to do it."

"Why don't you do it here?" Missy asked quickly. The way she asked, it was as if she thought it should have been obvious.

"Do you have a room that would work?" Holly asked. Rather than saying Brigid told her that Missy would probably offer it, she decided to see if she'd been right. Apparently, she was.

"Nobody really rents the room anymore, even though it's quite nice, so I just use it for storage for various things, but you can definitely use it. I have one or two people who use it through the year, but I haven't heard from them, so it's free." She gave Holly a careful look. "However, it does need to be cleaned out."

"That's not a problem," Holly said as she shook her head. "I don't have anything to do for a few hours. I could get started right away."

A knock on the door interrupted her. She paused, letting Missy handle it.

"I'm sorry," Missy said before speaking louder. "Come in."

The door opened and a girl who looked to be around Holly's age stepped in. Holly hadn't seen her around school, so she was instantly curious about her. The girl had very dark hair that was long and hanging in her face. She wore an olive-green military shirt over a black band tee shirt, but Holly couldn't read who it was. The girl glanced at Holly, but seemed to dismiss her at first glance. Her eyes lingered on Lucky sitting in Missy's lap.

"Do you need me to do anything today?" she grumbled. She rolled her eyes a bit as if she were forced to ask.

"Actually, I do. Holly here is going to be needing the rec room cleared out. You can go get started on it," Missy suggested. "I'll come help as soon as I can."

"Oh, that's okay," Holly began. She didn't know who this girl was, but she could tell she wasn't an eager helper. The last thing she needed was someone helping her who didn't want to. "I can do it myself."

"No, it's fine. Jada is helping me here for a few weeks, so I'm sure she'd be delighted," Missy said with a pointed look at the girl. She wasn't being demanding, but Holly could tell she was sending signals to the girl not to argue.

"Yeah, sure," the girl said as she turned around and left the room without another word.

"She really doesn't need to. I have time, and I could have done it myself," Holly said. It seemed as though Missy's request had irritated Jada.

"Jada's my niece," Missy explained. "She came to stay with us about a week ago. Unfortunately, her parents are having a rough time and they sent her to us while they work through a few things."

Missy sighed and leaned back in her chair. "But that girl is stubborn, not to mention that it seems she's mad at the world. And I can't say I really blame her. She's been having a tough time lately. I think she's become a bit of a pill in response."

"I'm sorry to hear that," Holly said. She couldn't imagine being sent to stay with your aunt while you waited to see if your parents were going to split up. It had to be a terribly stressful and upsetting time for her. "Maybe she'll come around?"

"I hope so," Missy sighed. "Because she's stressing Jordan and me out. We've seriously been discussing adopting children, but she's making us rethink it."

"Give her time," Holly said. "Sometimes people lash out when they're going through a tough time. Maybe she just feels like the only way to get attention is by acting out?" It wasn't as if Holly was immune to the stresses of being a teen. She knew exactly how frustrating it could be, feeling as though you're being held back when everyone tells you that you're not.

At times she had some of the same feelings, and she knew her friends did too. From her point of view, it was all a part of growing up. Parents thought they were doing their best to protect their kids while the kids struggled and fought against them, eager to gain their freedom and independence.

She had a feeling when she got older she'd understand the parents' side, but for now it just felt stifling. "I know plenty of kids at school who act the same way. It doesn't mean you're doing anything wrong."

"I swear, you're a wise old woman in a teenager's body," Missy said as she shook her head. She let Lucky jump down off of her lap before she stood up. "Come on, I'll help clean the room too."

CHAPTER THREE

Anymore, Jada Daniels felt as though she was always irritated. Maybe it was because she'd become disillusioned about her parents' problems. It was hard on her, no matter how much she tried to pretend otherwise. They may try to pretend like it's all going to be okay, but she knew better. It wasn't like she hadn't seen the same thing played out a thousand times. She'd been witness to her friends' parents getting divorced and she knew the warning signs.

It had all started when her mom had found something on her dad's phone. Jada wasn't sure exactly what it was, just that it had really upset her mom. After that, nothing was the same. For the first week or two they'd tried to hide the anger between them, but they didn't do a very good job of it. It was as plain as the foul expressions on their faces that they were mad at each other.

The tension between them was almost palpable any time they were in the same room together, which slowly became less and less. Soon the looks became hushed, angry whispers. After that, they stopped hiding it at all. Their arguments would crop up at the most random of times, and it didn't matter where they were. That was when they'd made the call to Missy to see if Jada could go to her aunt Missy's for a visit.

Flying alone from Baltimore to Denver, and then getting picked up at the airport, had been fairly uneventful. Some idle chit chat on the plane with the older woman that had been in the seat beside her, but that was about it. The hugs from Missy and Jordan when she'd arrived at the airport and they'd greeted her was also pretty routine.

It wasn't until they'd pulled into town that she realized just how small Cottonwood Springs really was. That was when she began to get angry. Why did she have to suffer in such a small town just because her parents couldn't keep it together? Maybe they were the ones who should have taken the trip and left her at home so she could live her life and spend time with her friends. Why did her life have to be put through the wringer because her parents weren't getting along? It wasn't fair.

Jada was frustrated as she pushed open the door to the rec room in the church. To be honest, she really didn't mind helping Missy and Jordan. They were good people and they had nothing to do with her parents and what was happening. They were just as much situational victims as she was.

But that hadn't stopped her from taking it out on them. She knew she was snappy with them and maybe even slightly cruel at times, but she couldn't help it. She was so upset with the way everything was going in her life that it was hard not to be. How could she be happy when she had no clue what was going on back home?

Jada had no idea what conclusions her parents had come to about their relationship and the family. She didn't know if they'd decided to split up or reconcile. She didn't know if she was going to be moving or if she'd get to stay where she'd lived most of her life. Her whole world could be unraveling back home, and she'd have no way of knowing. It just wasn't fair.

When she looked around the rec room, Jada noticed boxes of holiday decorations stacked in the back corner as well as a few more miscellaneous things that seemed to have been shoved into the room and forgotten about. She grabbed the nearest box and folded its flaps down before moving to the next one. They'd be easier to deal with if the flaps weren't hanging open.

She heard voices approach, and she sighed. She was doing her best to keep everyone at bay because, in her mind, it didn't do any good to make friends with anyone when she'd be going home soon. Why get close to someone or get to know these people? They lived half a country away. It wasn't like much of a friendship could come of it. If she kept her distance, it would make it easier when it was time to go home again.

"Here it is," Missy said as she pushed the door open. The blonde girl, Holly, who had been in Missy's office, followed her in. The little dog that Missy had been holding on her lap followed them as well, his nails clicking on the tile floor.

"This is perfect," Holly said with a grin. "And you're sure that nobody needs it?" She looked around the room as if it were the most incredible thing she'd ever seen. Jada rolled her eyes and picked up the closest box.

"If they did, they're too late now," Missy shrugged. "You need it, so you use it." Jada could tell that Missy was fond of this girl. She wondered what had brought the two together in the first place. Did Missy know this girl's mom and that was their relationship? But by the way they spoke to each other, it seemed like the two of them were friends.

"You really don't need to help," Holly said to Jada as their eyes met. The girl took a few steps towards her, almost as if she were curious.

"No, it's fine," Jada sighed. She wasn't mad about having to clean the room. Sometimes going through things could be fun. Besides, it helped kill the time. But she still had to act put out, because that way Missy wouldn't expect more from her.

Holly smiled, "I appreciate it." She turned and walked back to Missy's side. "I can already imagine all of the decorations up in here," she said, beaming as she looked around the room.

"Most of this stuff is supposed to be in the storage room. I admit, sometimes when I get the decorations this far, I just set them down and forget about them." Missy looked sheepish at the thought. "But by the time Jordan and I are done with whatever activity we had going on, we're often pretty beat and tired of looking at them," she said, chuckling.

"Oh really," Jada said, quietly mocking Missy under her breath. As if Missy had to apologize for being busy or not being able to be perfect all the time. She kind of liked Missy actually, but it drove Jada nuts that Missy was always doing everything all the time.

The woman never seemed to relax. If she ever did something that was remotely human, it seemed that she had to apologize for it. Deep down, she was hoping Missy would stop helping so many people all the time. She'd love to see Missy spend a day on the couch watching Netflix and eating pizza.

"I'm really excited for this party," Holly began as she started to pick up a box. "Now that I have a location, I plan on sending the email invites out today." She carried the box to the storage room and then came back out.

"I'm glad I could help," Missy said. "I have a key for this room. That way you can lock it up and keep your stuff safe," she began. "I usually keep the door to the church locked and then whoever has rented this room knows their things are safe."

"Okay, that sounds great," Holly said, nodding.

Jada listened to their exchange as she continued to collect boxes and carry them to the nearby storage room. It was the next room over, so it was easy to continue to eavesdrop.

Holly and Missy chatted about someone named Fiona and a clothing line. Apparently, Holly wanted to celebrate this person's accomplishments and throwing this party was a way to do that. Jada admitted to herself she was a bit jealous. She was barely able to get a birthday party, let alone a party to celebrate her accomplishments. The thought made Jada feel bitter and resentful.

As they finished moving boxes, and Jada grabbed a broom from the nearby closet, she continued to watch the two of them. If Jada was still being honest with herself, she had to admit it upset her to see how close Holly was to Missy.

They seemed to have forgotten she was even present as they moved around the room and continued to clean. She thought about slipping out of the door, figuring they'd never notice, but she was too busy listening to them, and the more she heard, the more she began to resent Holly. She wasn't sure why, but it was there, deep in her chest. It was like a brick, heavy, and weighing down her heart.

"Fiona has done so much for me," Holly was saying. "I just wanted to have the honor of throwing the party for her and letting her know how much she means to me."

"It's really sweet of you to do this for her," Missy said. "I don't know too many kids your age who would be willing to give up their hard-earned money to throw a party like this for someone. You're definitely going above and beyond."

That comment hurt Jada a little, even though she knew Missy was probably right. Would she be willing to spend a bunch of money on a party for someone who could afford to do it themselves? Probably not, but the fact that it was said that way still hurt. She was starting to think that Missy really had forgotten she was even there, which hurt even more.

"Do I need to do anything else?" Jada asked.

Missy and Holly turned, a surprised look on their faces. Either they really had forgotten she was there or her speaking just startled them.

"No, I think you did a fine job," Missy said with a kind smile. "Oh, would you grab one of the keys for the room for Holly? They're hanging up in my office. All of the duplicates are on the same hook, and they each have a little tag that says 'rec room' on them."

25

Jada nodded and hurried from the room. She couldn't wait to get as far away from Missy and Holly as possible. She seemed like a goody-goody, the kind of girl that Jada and her friends would pick on back home.

"Man, I wish my friends were here," Jada sighed as she opened the door to Missy's office and stepped in. "They could help me have a little fun."

Spotting the keys, she paused as she took the first key off the hook. Maybe her friends weren't here to help her stir things up, but that didn't mean she couldn't do it on her own. Maybe this little party needed to hit a few speed bumps. And perhaps those speed bumps might just derail the party all together. That thought made Jada smile as she wrapped her fingers around the key and returned to where Missy and Holly were in the rec room.

"Here you go," she said sweetly as she handed the key over.

"Thanks," Holly said. "I really appreciate it."

"Oh, it's no problem," Jada said, giving her a sugary sweet smile. She didn't want to let on that she was feeling any animosity towards Holly. Yet as she looked at Holly, she saw Holly pause and seem to really look at her.

Caught off guard, Jada turned. "Well if you don't need anything else, I'm going to go get on my phone," she said casually.

"You may want to check with Jordan," Missy said as Jada hurried towards the door. "He mentioned he might need some help."

"I'd love to," Jada said sarcastically before stepping out into the hall. Rather than turning towards Jordan's office, she headed towards her room. There was no way she was doing anything else today. She had to figure out how to sabotage a party.

CHAPTER FOUR

The following day, Brigid asked, "Have you heard back from anyone yet?" They were getting ready to go order food for the party, and Holly was brushing her hair before they left.

"Yes, and I'm really surprised," Holly said. "I can't believe how many responses I've already gotten. I'm glad there's going to be so many people, but I have to admit it's a little nerve-wracking." She set the brush down on the coffee table and turned to Brigid. "I'm ready when you are."

"Why's that?" Brigid asked as they headed out of the front door.

"It's just so many people," Holly sighed. "I knew it was a lot when I sent out the invite. I put a flyer up at the bookstore when I knew Fiona would be gone asking people to leave their email addresses if they wanted to be a part of celebrating Fiona's accomplishments. Before I knew it, my paper was full, and I had to replace it a couple of times. For some reason, I almost expected people to change their minds. Anyway, so far I have something close to fifty people who have said they'll come."

"It will all work out," Brigid reassured her. "It may seem intimidating at first, but don't worry. Everyone who comes will be more focused on celebrating Fiona than anything else," she said as they drove through town, heading for the grocery store.

"But what if people think the decorations are too immature or something?" Holly fretted. It was something she'd been worried about, having people think it was obvious a kid had done the decorating.

"I've seen some of the things you've chosen, and I think it's going to look great. Why would anyone think a kid did the decorating?" Brigid asked. "I'm sure you're overthinking this whole thing," she said as she pulled into the grocery store parking lot.

It was called Willard's and was owned by a local family. They always tried to shop at local stores rather than at big chain stores, even if sometimes it cost a little bit more. Brigid had preached to Holly frequently how important it was to understand and support small businesses.

"Maybe you're right," Holly admitted. Even so, she could sense the feelings of anxiety creeping up whenever she thought about it. "I just want to make sure the party is perfect for Fiona. I don't want to mess it up for her."

They climbed out of the car and approached the store. Each window had a huge advertisement for this week's specials. Holly watched as Brigid checked them out before Brigid turned back to her.

"You can do it," she said with conviction. "It may seem daunting, but if you encounter any snags, I know you can handle them. Remember that it's just a party. What you're doing is a good thing, so don't let fear hold you back."

Holly knew Brigid was right. As they walked through the automatic doors, Holly decided then and there that no matter what issues might crop up, she'd handle them. She was well aware that not many planned things went off without a hitch, so she was afraid that with a party this size, any problem might be insurmountable. But she made her mind up that she wouldn't give up.

Fiona really did deserve this, and Holly wanted to be the one to give it to her. Besides, worrying about something that hadn't happened was ridiculous. She'd learned long ago that her imagination often made her think that people thought less of her than they really did. This was probably one of those situations. She just had to keep things in perspective, no matter what.

They walked to the back of the store where the deli counter was located and stopped to look up at the prices. Together they debated the various selections under the catering section. Holly had no idea what she should get or how much, which was why she'd asked Brigid to come along. This was all new territory for her, and she knew she needed some help from someone with experience.

"I think you should get some finger sandwiches and a couple of deli trays," Brigid suggested. They'd gone over all of the options, but these seemed to be the best. "That way there will be some food, but nothing needs to be kept warm or fussed over. Simple, classy, and versatile. Plus, it will be less stress for you."

"If you say so," Holly shrugged. It sounded as good as anything she could come up with. Besides, if it was something that was no stress and easy to work with, all the better.

"Brigid, is that you?" a woman's voice asked from behind them. Holly didn't recognize the voice, and she looked at Brigid.

Brigid turned and a surprised expression swept across her face. "Jodi?" Brigid gasped, surprised. "I thought you moved to Minnesota?" She and the woman gave each other a polite little hug.

"I did," the woman said. Her close-cropped hair was starting to go gray at the temples, and her lips were pursed as if she were always pondering something. She had a basket looped over her arm, and she gave off the air of someone who would look down her nose at others. Holly wasn't impressed. "I moved back about a month ago."

"Wow, that's great," Brigid gushed. Holly could tell by Brigid's tone that she was being polite. She'd never heard of her before, so Holly wasn't so sure this woman was someone Brigid and Fiona were actually fond of.

"Jodi, this is my daughter Holly. Holly, this is Jodi. She was Fiona's best friend through most of school and then beyond, if I remember correctly." Brigid introduced the two and they politely said hello to one another. Holly didn't want to be rude, but she didn't want to stand around and talk to this woman at the moment. She had more important things to do.

"Well, not quite beyond," Jodi shrugged. "We had a bit of a falling out before I moved away," she admitted. She looked down at the floor and fidgeted nervously with her basket.

"No one agrees all the time," Brigid said, seemingly oblivious to the woman's nervousness. Holly wondered if maybe she was passing judgment a little too quickly, and this woman was just like this all the time. "We're here getting food for a party to celebrate Fiona." Brigid grinned happily, as if her sister's successes were her own.

"It's not her birthday," Jodi stated as she wrinkled her brow, confused.

"Oh, no," Holly interjected. "It's a party to celebrate her clothing line." She was proud to share Fiona's accomplishment.

Jodi blinked, obviously surprised. "She has a clothing line?" Her eyes darted from Brigid to Holly and then back again. She seemed stunned to be out of the loop.

"You haven't heard?" Brigid asked. When Jodi shook her head, eyes wide, she continued. "She's taken time away from the bookstore in order to try her hand at fashion design. You probably remember how much she loved it when she was in school."

"Well, she started putting her designs on social media and ended up catching a lot of attention. She was offered a deal with a clothing manufacturer, and her first line should be coming out soon." Brigid grinned, clearly proud of her sister. As she should be.

"Wow," Jodi said, clearly shocked. "Well, I guess good for her." Her words sounded like they were encouraging, but her tone was definitely not. It was flat, lacking any real emotion. Holly studied the woman, wondering what the deal was with her. If she and Fiona had once been friends, she'd think Jodi would be happy for her. The fact that she didn't seem that way made Holly raise one eyebrow in curiosity.

"We're so incredibly proud of her," Brigid continued, not noticing the woman's odd behavior or perhaps simply choosing to ignore it. "It's such an amazing accomplishment."

"It certainly sounds like it," Jodi said with a forced smile. "I hate to chat and run, but I have a lot to do and still need to grab a few things. Maybe we can catch up sometime later?"

Brigid nodded and the two women said their goodbyes before Jodi disappeared down an aisle. Holly watched her leave and then turned to Brigid. "What's her deal? She seems a little strange. You said she was Fiona's friend, but it sure didn't seem that way to me."

"Oh, don't worry about her," Brigid said in a dismissive manner. "She and Fiona were always back and forth with each other. One day they'd hate each other, and the next day they'd be friends again. I wouldn't worry about it. I'm sure it's nothing."

Holly nodded, but she wasn't so sure. It seemed to her that Jodi didn't react well to the news that Fiona was getting attention. If she were to guess, she'd guess that Jodi was upset by it. But she'd only met the woman for a few moments, and Brigid had known her for a long time. She'd know if Jodi's behavior was odd. Instead of worrying about something that had no bearing on the present, she pushed her thoughts of Jodi aside and returned her focus to the deli counter.

"If you'd like, I can go ahead and order these," Brigid told Holly. "Why don't you go pick out a couple of those take and bake pizzas? We'll have those for dinner tonight."

Holly nodded. "Those are Linc's favorite," she said with a smile.

"I know," Brigid said with a wink. "I thought we'd surprise him."

Holly nodded and began to walk across the store to the cooler that held the pizzas. Now that they were getting the food order, Holly was almost ready for the party. She had everything scheduled to be picked up the day before the party, so she'd be set up and ready for the big day.

She'd need to have someone pick up the cake on the day of the party, though. Holly was scheduled to work with Fiona that day and that worked out perfectly for her plans, because she could make sure Fiona didn't notice anything. Holly had decided to try to make the party a surprise and so far, it seemed to be working.

Fiona was so preoccupied with making sure everything was perfect for the clothing line and at the bookstore, it was almost as if she were in another world most of the time. Holly had told everyone that the party was a surprise, and it seemed that no one had spilled the beans. So far, so good.

Just as she came to a stop in front of the pizza cooler, her phone began to ring. She took it out of her pocket and saw that it was Wade, her longtime boyfriend.

"Hey," she said with a smile as she answered.

"You sound like you're in a good mood," he said.

"I'm getting the last things for the party ordered," she explained. "Almost in the home stretch."

"Good for you," he said happily. "So what are you doing tomorrow night?"

Holly searched her brain but couldn't think of anything. 'Nothing that I can think of," she said.

"Then I'd like for us to go out. How does that sound? I'll take you to dinner."

"Great, what time?" she asked.

"I'll pick you up around 6:00," he said. "We won't be out too late since we have school the next day, but I felt like doing something spontaneous in the middle of the week." Holly could hear by his voice he was excited. She wondered why he sounded so happy about it when they did this sort of thing all the time on the weekends. But rather than pick it apart, she decided to just go with it.

"Sounds like a date," she said before they hung up. Leaning over, she picked out a couple of pizzas and turned to go find Brigid.

CHAPTER FIVE

Jodi Young did not take the news of Fiona's success well. It was true that at one time she and Fiona had been very close. When they were in grade school, they used to spend the night at each other's house all the time. But over the years, as they got older, Jodi often found herself resentful of Fiona.

From Jodi's perspective, Fiona was blessed beyond measure, whereas she was not. It seemed like it had always been that way, even when they were young. When she'd moved back to Cottonwood Springs, she'd hoped that things had changed with Fiona, but she was beginning to think they hadn't. Just hearing about Fiona and her accomplishments made her so mad she could spit.

Jodi had been telling everyone that her husband and son would be joining her soon in Cottonwood Springs, but that was a lie. In reality, neither one of them ever wanted to speak to her again after she'd done a little too much online shopping. She'd accidentally spent the money for their house payment and the utilities, leaving them in a bad place.

It wasn't like she'd planned on doing that, but when all the charges she'd run up had been paid through their checking account at the bank, it was almost depleted. It wasn't the first time it had happened, and her husband had finally asked her to leave. He'd told her that he'd had enough, and he couldn't go through it again.

She'd known she shouldn't do it, but she couldn't help herself. When she found good deals, it was almost impossible for her to pass them up. But with nowhere to go and out of work, she moved back to her old hometown where things were cheaper and she could live in her parent's old house that a renter had recently vacated.

Thinking back on the last fight she'd had with Fiona, Jodi wasn't blind to the fact she'd said some pretty hurtful things, but it was just after Fiona had opened her bookstore, and Jodi was going to be moving away. She'd wanted Fiona to listen to her and stop talking about her bookstore, but she couldn't or maybe she simply wouldn't.

In the end, Jodi had blown up at her and refused to speak to her ever again. So far, she hadn't. She knew it had been childish and petty of her, but her feelings had been hurt. All she'd wanted was for her friend to be happy for her instead of droning on and on about one more thing she was doing. Jodi was sure it was yet another brilliant thing Fiona would be praised for, and she couldn't take it anymore.

And she'd been right. Fiona had created something of an icon in Cottonwood Springs. A place where people could hang out and bond over a good book. It seemed as though everyone loved "Read It Again," and some people had taken up reading again just because of her store.

Jodi had to admit that was pretty cool, but the fact of the matter was that it just made her feel like more of a failure. She never would have thought that bonding over book circles and a cup of coffee could bring people together like that.

Pulling into her driveway, Jodi grabbed her bag of groceries and hurried into the house. It still felt odd walking through the door again and living there, but she was slowly getting used to it. She'd been back for a couple of weeks now, and while she still missed her home and family, she'd started finding a new normal here.

Jodi had been numb for a while after her husband had kicked her out, walking through life as if she were in a daze. But this news about Fiona took things to a whole different level. How could this be her life? How could Fiona end up with everything, while Jodi was left with nothing? She had no family, a sad excuse for a job, and she was living in her parent's old house.

It was as though her entire life had been ripped out from under her, all while Fiona was having a fashion line handed to her on a silver platter. It wasn't fair. What had she ever done to deserve this?

Jodi set her bag of groceries down on the counter and began to unload her meager purchases. She couldn't plan a party even if she wanted to, and she was fairly sure nobody would want to come anyway. Even though people had seemed friendly when she'd seen them around town, nobody had taken the time to visit her. She'd been seriously considering seeing a counselor. Someone to help her process all the things that were happening around her and to her, because she didn't feel capable enough to handle everything on her own.

After she'd put everything away, she realized she was still in a foul mood. Just knowing there was going to be a celebration for Fiona got under her skin. It was like an itch she couldn't scratch, an irritation that wouldn't go away. And with no friends or family around to help ease her pain, it only seemed to fester. And to add insult to injury, she hadn't even been invited to the party. How fair was that?

Apparently Brigid didn't know that she and Fiona weren't friends anymore, so why hadn't Brigid extended an invitation to her? It had been obvious she lived in Cottonwood Springs now. She'd had plenty of opportunities to invite Jodi when she was going on and on about how great Fiona was.

She didn't want to hear any more about how great Fiona was, she just wanted an invite to the party. But that hadn't happened. Instead, Jodi was left feeling shut out, and she couldn't stop wondering why she hadn't been invited to attend the party.

Jodi went into the living room and flopped down on the couch. She sighed and then said to herself, "Actually, it's pretty obvious that they don't want me at their perfect little party. Why would they invite someone they didn't even like?" She tucked her feet beneath her.

She had always felt like Brigid's niceness was just an act. No one could possibly be that happy and sweet all the time. She always seemed to be willing to listen to others, no matter what she had going on at the moment. In school, she'd been older than Jodi, but Jodi had seen her enough to remember what she'd been like.

"I know a fake person when I see one," she grumbled as she turned on the TV. She was sure anyone who was that positive all the time had to be a fake. No one was that happy. Life happened to everyone, and if someone ever said that it didn't beat them down from time to time, she knew they were lying. Maybe Brigid was just good at pretending, but Jodi couldn't stand it anymore. She couldn't bring herself to pretend it was all okay, so nobody else should be able to either.

Trying to distract herself with some mindless TV show, she flipped through the channels, looking for something that could take her mind off of things for a while. She wanted to escape from reality and everything that was in it. The world had become such an unfair place.

She got lost in an episode of reality TV, allowing herself to be distracted by other people's problems. That was probably one of her favorite things about reality TV. You could watch other people collapse and lose their cool all while being in the comfort of your own home. It was nice to see that others had problems that they didn't know how to cope with, too. Things seemed a little fairer that way.

As she became engrossed in a couple of women fighting, the ringing of her phone pulled her back to reality. Picking it up, she saw it was one of her only friends here in Cottonwood Springs. Becky had been a friend to her the entire time. There was no jealousy and no bragging between them.

It seemed like Becky was the one person in the world who understood Jodi. They often came to the same conclusions about the people around them, making it even easier for them to bond. They talked at length about other people's lives and their poor choices.

"Hey," she said as she answered the phone. At least she had Becky to talk to. That helped make things easier.

"What are you up to?" Becky asked. It sounded like she was crunching on potato chips.

"Just watching TV, trying to understand why I have absolutely no luck, and Fiona has it all," she said as she watched the women on TV swinging at each other.

"What do you mean?" Becky asked. It was strange how she never seemed to know what was going on in Cottonwood Springs, but then again, she had four kids that kept her busy, and she didn't work. She was always a little more out of the loop than Jodi, which was kind of nice. She may have been in Cottonwood Springs the whole time Jodi had been gone, but she never knew the best gossip.

Jodi began to explain what happened at the store and explained the new stroke of luck that Fiona seemed to have had come her way. She told her friend all about the party and how she hadn't been invited, even though Brigid and Holly had been quick to tell her about it. "Ugh, I can't stand it," she finished. "It just makes me want to pull my hair out."

"Wouldn't it be funny if her party was wrecked?" Becky asked. "Like things just started happening to mess it all up. Like when you make reservations, but the place loses them or the caterer writes down the wrong day. If that happened, I bet it would make you feel better."

Jodi knew Becky was being flippant about the whole thing, but the thought made Jodi smile. "That would be pretty great," she sighed. She could just imagine it. For once, something not going Fiona's way. It would be like karma was finally catching up to her. If only it were possible.

"Don't let it get to you," Becky said, bringing Jodi back from her short-lived fantasy. "You know that good things come to those who wait. Just do what you have to get your feet back under you. Your good luck time will come as long as you keep on the straight and narrow. Show your husband you can control your spending and know what a budget is, then your life can get back to normal. Don't give Fiona a second thought."

There were sounds in the background and Becky said. "I have to go. I need to go play chauffeur again. I'll talk to you later."

Jodi hung up, but Becky's words were still echoing in her mind. The idea of Fiona's party getting ruined caused a giddy feeling she hadn't had for quite a while. Yet she knew she couldn't just cross her fingers and hope that the party was ruined. No, she'd have to take matters into her own hands. She'd have to come up with ways to make sure this party didn't happen. But could she do it? Could she manage to disrupt the party being given for Fiona?

It might take some ingenuity, but she was fairly sure if she put her mind to it, she could accomplish it. She'd never been a quitter, and she didn't plan on starting now. When she decided to do something, she'd see it through to the end. Now, what could she do to start?

CHAPTER SIX

Holly couldn't believe how nice it was to go to dinner with Wade on their date night. They hadn't been on one for a while now, what with work, school, and occasionally tutoring. But it had been just as nice as it was the first time they'd gone together. He never failed to make her feel special. Wade always knew just the right things to do and say at any given time. It was almost as if he were a mind reader.

Once they'd finished dinner, they made their way out of their favorite restaurant, Wahoo's, a Mexican restaurant that specialized in fish tacos, without saying a word. They were walking to his car, hand in hand, and she couldn't help but smile. It had been a great evening. Just relaxing and being teenagers for a few hours. The way their schedules were, sometimes it felt as if they already were grown-ups.

"What?" he asked when they got to the passenger side of his car. He opened the door for her and had noticed her smile, and she stood there for a minute.

"I'm just happy," she said, continuing to smile. She leaned closer to him and gave him a small kiss on the cheek. He seemed surprised at the gesture and then grinned. Once she saw that she'd made him just as happy as she was, she got in the car. She tucked her legs in the car, and he shut her door and went around to his side.

When he was in the car, he turned and looked at her. "I'm glad you're happy," he said as he shut his door "because I'm happy, too. It's been a great night, and the dinner was great."

Holly nodded. "So now what are we doing?" she asked. Wade had told her that the rest of their date night was going to be a surprise, but she thought he might give her a clue or something. Just a little hint to keep her guessing.

"I think I'll leave you in suspense," he said with a grin. "If that's okay with you?" She could tell by his apprehensive look he didn't want to upset her.

"Sure," she said. "I trust your judgment." If he wanted to keep it a surprise, who was she to complain?

Wade pulled out of the parking space and turned on some soft music as he drove. Holly stared out of the window, watching the cars go by and people walking on the sidewalk. It was a nice evening and people seemed to be taking advantage of it.

"I honestly can't imagine my life without you. I remember in the beginning being so nervous when we were in the library, I could barely even ask you to tutor me," he admitted.

Holly remembered those days. It seemed like it was long ago. It may have only been a couple of years, but her life had changed so much since then, it almost felt like a lifetime had gone by.

"Seriously?" she asked, surprised. "But why? I'm just me." She'd always felt as though she wasn't anything special. Just an average girl in a big world.

"That's exactly why," he said as he slowed down for a stoplight. "Because you're you. You're so smart, confident, and capable. Even when you were going through the chaos with your mom and then after she was murdered it was like you were this strong and competent person, and I didn't see how you could be interested in someone like me. I am just a jock who sometimes struggles with his classes."

41

Holly could hear from the tone of Wade's voice how much he believed that. He was being serious, baring his heart to her. He was telling her what it had been like from his perspective, and it was eye-opening to her. She'd never expected to hear anyone describe her in that way.

"Believe me, that wasn't what it was like from my point of view," she said. "It's true that before my mom died, I saw things differently. I didn't think anyone would want anything to do with me. I was just trailer trash, you know? I had a couple of friends, but we weren't close. Mainly because I couldn't do anything after school with them. I was too embarrassed to invite anyone to my home.

"People would ask me to their home, but when I didn't reciprocate, the invitations eventually ended. I just thought I'd do what I could to make it through high school. I never expected to have real friends or a boyfriend."

"They didn't know what was happening," Wade said. "Kids don't understand things like that. We were all too young to really grasp what you were dealing with when you went home. The things you had to do, far too much for someone your age to deal with."

"Yeah, maybe," she admitted. "But it didn't make things any easier at the time. I was the one living that life, and I had no one to talk to and nowhere to really turn, except a few adults who knew and kept me sane. Like Missy."

"I'm sure it didn't make things easier," he said. "But I really don't think anyone did it to deliberately hurt you."

Holly fell silent as she watched the sun slipping behind the mountains in the distance. It was odd how a little bit of perspective could change everything. It was easy to be able to look back and see how things really were, but at the time, her feelings had been much different.

She'd often felt like the whole town was talking about her behind her back. Whispering about how pathetic she was. She remembered wishing she were old enough to get away from Cottonwood Springs and everyone in it. Now she was glad she hadn't.

Wade kept driving and Holly did her best to try to guess where they were going. Was he taking her to the bowling alley? Or maybe the skating rink? There weren't a whole lot of things to do in Cottonwood Springs. She waited to see where he was going to turn in, but then she realized they were leaving town.

"Now I'm really curious where we're going," Holly said. "What do you have up your sleeve?" she asked.

"We're almost there. Then I promise, you'll understand. Just a little longer," he said calmly. It was almost as if he had read her mind, knowing she'd be curious as to what he was up to. Holly nodded and continued to stare out the window.

Wade pulled off on a gravel road and slowed the car. "I found this place a little while ago, and I really wanted to bring you here, but I wanted it to be special when I did. I don't know, I was afraid you might think it was silly," he said as the last of the sun dipped below the mountains.

"No, I understand," Holly said. She'd seen a few places like that before. Like special nature spots that seemed almost as if they'd been created for someone to enjoy.

"Right," he said, nodding. He slowed when they came to the top of a hill and pulled off on the shoulder. There was a small pull-off area where there was no grass. It had been worn down and now the area was just bare dirt and rocks.

Looking out, Holly could see why. The hill was high up and looked out over an expanse of flat area. You could see the lights of a nearby town twinkling in the distance as the sky turned a blazing orange that faded into purples and then eventually stars on the opposite side of the sky. It was a stunning view, and she couldn't believe she'd never seen it before.

"How did you find this?" she asked softly. It was so beautiful it seemed as though it was only appropriate to speak quietly.

"I was running an errand for work and stumbled across it," he said as he looked at the view. "Come on, this isn't the only thing." He opened his door and climbed out, popping the trunk as he went. He walked back to the trunk and pulled out a blanket which he carried to the nearby field. He fluffed it out and then let it drift gently down to the grass.

"Won't we get in trouble for being here?" Holly asked as she looked around for a house. It was clearly someone's property, and she didn't want to be caught trespassing. It might be a romantic spot, but it wouldn't be very romantic if they were run off. Especially if whoever owned the land wasn't nice.

"Honest, it's fine. Stop worrying so much," he said with a smile before returning to the trunk of his car. "Just sit on the blanket and relax."

Holly nodded and sat down cross-legged. She didn't like feeling as though they were doing something wrong, but then she took a deep breath. They weren't going to leave any trash or tear anything up.

If the owner didn't drive by while they were there, they'd have no way of knowing Holly and Wade were on their property. She watched as Wade pulled a guitar from the trunk. "You know how to play?" she asked, surprised.

"I've been learning," he admitted. "I wanted it to be a surprise."

"That's amazing," she said happily. "You'll have to show me how."

"Sure," he said, closing the trunk. He looked nervous as he came to join her, and she grinned. She felt so lucky to have a boyfriend like Wade. She knew that other girls would love to have him as their boyfriend. How could they not? He'd matured a lot in their time together, and his once lanky body had filled out. Now he was tall and broad shouldered with long dark lashes that made his eyes irresistible.

As he settled on the blanket, Wade made sure his guitar was in tune before finally starting to strum. When he began to play, she recognized the song. It was a slow song about a boy's love for a girl and hoping they could always be together. She'd never heard him sing before and to hear his voice now brought tears to her eyes.

His brow was furrowed as he concentrated at first, but then he grew comfortable with the song, and his voice became a little louder and clearer. By the time he finished the song, she had to brush tears from her eyes. She couldn't stop smiling.

"Wade, that was beautiful," she said softly.

He began to dig in his pocket, pulling out a little box.

"I want to make you a promise, Holly," he said. "I want you to know how much you mean to me and how committed I am to you." He opened the lid of the box and in the dim light she could see a twinkle and she gasped.

"This is a promise ring," he explained. "I know people don't really do these anymore, but I like the idea. This ring is a promise to you that I'm serious about our relationship. It's like a pre-engagement ring. It lets you know that while we may be too young to get married right now, I'm hoping we can in the future. It's my promise to you."

If Holly hadn't been crying tears of joy before, she certainly was now. "Oh my gosh, Wade," she sobbed. "I love it!"

He pulled the ring out of the box and slipped it on her finger, the same one where wedding rings go. Setting the guitar to the side, he leaned forward and pulled her close. His lips met hers and it was a gentle and tender expression of his love.

"I love you," he said with all the sincerity and devotion a person could give another.

"I love you too," she said softly.

CHAPTER SEVEN

Michelle Owens pulled into the church parking lot, ready to finalize her plans. Every year she was in charge of organizing her family's reunion, and this year was no different. She'd ordered all the decorations and sent out the invites, now she just had to nail down the rec room at the church. Not that it would be an issue, because she used it every year at this time, and Missy knew that.

Michelle felt like she should practically have the room reserved indefinitely. If she could just have that agreement and then always have the key to the room, it would make this whole thing much easier. It would be one less thing to do. Instead, every year she had to come and talk to Missy.

Not that she really minded. After all, she spoke with Missy all the time after church services or around town when they'd bump into each other. They may not get together on the weekends or anything like that, but they were on good terms.

She'd actually meant to bring up the room to Missy when she saw her last Sunday after the church service, but Missy had been busy speaking with people and she never had the opportunity. Plus, Michelle's husband had been anxious to get home and get ready for the football game, so they'd left. She'd kicked herself for it ever since.

However, today she knew she couldn't put it off. She needed to get the key, so she could start bringing stuff in and getting organized. Right now she had everything in her bedroom, and Michelle was eager to gain her space back.

This wasn't the first time she'd waited until the last minute to reserve the room. Two years ago, she'd been very sick and hadn't been able to get to it until the last minute. But it had all worked out well, so she was confident this year would be the same.

She climbed out of her car, grabbed her purse, and pulled her cardigan around her. It was sunny out, but a slight breeze made her feel chilled, and she wondered if she should have worn a jacket instead.

Can't get sick, she thought. *I have way too much to do. I'll make sure I take some elderberry syrup when I get home.*

Rounding the side of the church, she noticed that they'd recently put new mulch down in the flower beds. Michelle took a moment to look closely at them and appreciate their work. She made a mental note to ask Jordan what they used to keep the weeds out. She was forever trying to find something to keep them from popping through her mulch at home, but it seemed like no matter what she used, she lost the battle.

As she made her way to the front of the church, the warmth of the sun made a smile spread across her face. Today was going to be a great day to do everything. She'd get the key from Missy, then head home and grab her stuff. With all the paid time off she'd built up at work, she'd decided to take the week off.

It was nice to know that this year she wouldn't have to wait until the last minute. Entering the church from the front, she saw Missy vacuuming the carpet in the aisles of the chapel. The sound of the vacuum echoed off the high ceilings, but that didn't keep Missy from hearing the sound of the heavy wooden door closing behind Michelle.

"Well, hello, Michelle," Missy said happily as she shut off the vacuum. "I'm so glad you came to visit." She took a few steps toward the woman, glad for a reason to take a break.

"Me, too. It feels like it's been a while since we could visit with each other. I meant to speak with you on Sunday, but you were a little preoccupied," Michelle said as she tossed her wavy brown hair over her shoulder.

"Aren't I always?" Missy laughed. She turned and looked at a nearby pew and gestured towards it. "Come, sit. We have so much to talk about. It seems like we haven't chatted in forever."

"How are things with your niece?" Michelle asked. "I knew she was coming, but I hadn't heard anything since." She had important business to discuss, but waiting a little while for some friendly conversation wouldn't be the end of the world. Once in a while it was nice to just catch up with people.

Missy looked conflicted before answering. "I know she's a good kid at heart, but she's in pain," she said as she bit her lip. "I've tried talking to her, but it seems like the more I try, the more she pulls away. She's moody and short-tempered. She doesn't want to do anything or go anywhere, and I'm beginning to feel like I'm holding her hostage."

"She's a teenager," Michelle shrugged. "I wouldn't take it too personally. She's probably got a lot on her mind. And I'm sure it has nothing to do with you. I've known a few to act like that even when they're with their parents."

"I'm sure," Missy nodded. "The poor thing. She doesn't know that some nights we can hear her softly crying through the door of her room. I feel for her, I really do, but she's making things very difficult."

"How so?" Michelle asked.

"She's fiercely independent," Missy began. "She disappears, and we have no clue where she goes. I don't know if she's getting in trouble or what. I half expect Sheriff Davis to show up with her in tow someday. She didn't use to be like this."

"Kids change," Michelle said. "Especially teenage girls. One day they're sweet and precious and then another day they hate your guts. It's a strange thing, but it's true."

"Surely, not all teens," Missy said as she paled a little.

"No, not all," Michelle said. "But there are always struggles. Try not to take her rebellion to heart. Considering the situation, I'm sure it has nothing to do with you. Good grief, I still have hormonal days where I can be hard to live with."

Missy sighed. "Okay, good. I'm trying, but I wasn't so sure I could manage. But once you put it into perspective like that, I can see your point. Just when she's trying to figure out her place in the world, her world has come crashing down. She's got her own thing going on internally and then she's got her parents and Jordan and me. That would be a lot for anyone to handle."

"You've got this," Michelle said kindly. If anyone had the patience to help the girl, it would be Missy. She was always incredibly honest and forthright. The girl couldn't keep her defenses forever. Missy was the kind of person that was relentlessly nice. You just can't stay mad at someone like that forever.

"Enough talk about me," Missy said, brightening a bit. "What have you been up to? Anything special or exciting going on?" It made Michelle happy just to see how interested Missy always was in her. It was something she did with everyone. If she had a conversation with you, she'd make you feel as if you were the only person in the world and she was completely focused on you. And she truly was.

"Not too much," she sighed. "You know how it goes. Day in and day out, same old, same old." It frustrated her that it was that way, but sometimes there was no time for fun. At least there hadn't been for a while. "But I took the whole week off. Every year when I plan the family reunion, I end up worn-out and frazzled by the time the day comes. The days seem shorter and work takes longer. So I thought I'd give myself a little break and take some days off that I'd saved up."

"Good for you!" Missy cheered. "That's what I like to hear. Sometimes we have to put self-care first or we'll burn out. If you ask me, I think half the population lives that way anymore. You know, running on empty and completely spent." She shook her head. "Breaks my heart."

"It is terrible, isn't it?" Michelle agreed. "All that just to get money to pay our bills. Anyway, I'm getting off track. I came here for a reason."

"Okay," Missy agreed. "What do you need?"

"It's that time of year again," she said. "The family reunion is drawing closer, and I need to grab the key to the rec room, so I can get ready for this weekend. No more last-minute decorating and throwing things together. I swore I'd do better this year, but so far I'm not." She laughed nervously.

"Oh," Missy said, her face falling. "I'm afraid I can't do that."

Michelle felt her heart drop into her stomach. "What do you mean? I can't use the rec room?" She was sure this had to be a little joke that Missy was playing on her. Why wouldn't she let her use it? Nobody else ever did.

"Not this weekend," Missy said, looking saddened. "I'm letting someone else use it this weekend. I'm really sorry, I didn't know. But you can have it next weekend."

"But I've already told everyone it would be here this weekend," Michelle sputtered. Her mind was reeling as she tried to make sense of this. She'd never had a problem before and now she was caught in a bind. There was no way she could have the reunion at her home. There wasn't enough room. Was there even anywhere else to hold it? And would she be able to reserve it on such short notice?

"I'm sorry," Missy shrugged. "I didn't know. Someone else wanted to use it, and I've already given them the key. If she changes her mind, I'll let you know."

Michelle could feel her anger boiling up, but she quickly tamped it down. "Okay, thanks. That would be great. Until then, I guess I need to make some changes," she said, but she really didn't want to. She began thinking about how she could get the other person to let her use the room. Perhaps if they could be convinced... "Who was it, by the way?"

"Holly Lewis," Missy said. "She's throwing a party for her aunt Fiona."

"Fiona that owns the bookstore?" Michelle asked.

"That's the one," Missy nodded. "She's already done all the legwork of getting a cake and food from the local deli. I doubt anything is going to change, just so you know."

Michelle nodded. "I understand," she said quickly. Standing, she wiped her hands on her shirt. They'd suddenly become damp. "I guess I better get going, I have a lot of work to do."

"Swing by after this weekend, and I'll give you the key," Missy said. "You can use it any other time."

"I will," Michelle said as she turned and hurried out of the church.

For a moment, she considered what she'd need to do to reschedule, but she hated the thought. What if people couldn't come because they were used to it being on this one weekend? No, she needed another plan. One that would free up the rec room at the church, so that she could use it instead of Holly. Her family reunion was more important anyway. What had Fiona done recently that warranted a big party? Nothing she was aware of.

Hurrying to her car, Michelle climbed behind the wheel and shut the door. She was about to start the engine, but realized she needed a moment before she'd be able to drive. Her hands were shaking and there was some sort of emotion coursing through her veins. She wasn't sure if it was anger, panic, or something else altogether. Whatever it was, it made her feel desperate. She'd do anything not to have to change her plans, even if that meant sabotaging someone else's party.

CHAPTER EIGHT

Jenny Crabtree stood in her boutique store and smiled. She'd come a long way from her humble beginnings. Starting a clothing store in a little town like Cottonwood Springs was a risky venture, but so far it seemed as though it had paid off.

She'd always felt like she was meant to be someone. Someone important, at least in town. Now, she felt like she was. She had all the right connections, and she was moving up in the world. Only those people in Cottonwood Springs with the most money were her customers.

Of course, sometimes those who didn't have as much liked to come in and browse, but she could spot them a mile away. Their eyes bulged out when they saw a price tag. Those weren't her ideal customers. No, her store aimed for a much higher clientele.

Now she was looking to expand and give her shop, "Chic Boutique," a little more notoriety. It was time to be more than just A clothing store in Cottonwood Springs. She wanted to be THE clothing store. And she wanted to have something that other places didn't have, like jewelry and clothing that couldn't be found in other stores. That would cause people from all over the area to come and visit her store.

Maybe then she'd be able to consider herself a success, but until that happened, she still felt as though her business was on shaky ground. She may have the higher-end customers in Cottonwood Springs, but that wasn't good enough. She wanted them to come from as far away as Denver.

The bell over the door tinkled, and she looked up to see Fiona Garcia enter.

"Fiona, hi!" she said happily. "How are you doing?" She and Fiona weren't best friends or anything, but she felt they were on fairly good terms. She knew the woman was business smart and going places, so it paid to stay on good terms with her. You just never know when having connections could be a benefit in the long run.

"I'm doing great," Fiona said with a smile. "I came in to see if you'd gotten in anything new that I can't live without. You know how it goes." She headed to the rack where Jenny displayed the newest additions to her store. The regulars loved it because then they could find it all in one place. It also seemed to boost her sales.

"You'd look good in that cute cardigan," Jenny suggested as she came around from behind the counter. She knew Fiona tended to like cardigans, scarves, and accessories.

Fiona held it up in front of the nearby full-length mirror. "You think?" she asked as she looked at her reflection. "I really like what this color does for my hair." She continued to turn from side to side, observing herself in the mirror.

"That shade of green is really flattering on you," Jenny observed, and it wasn't a lie. Fiona was very pretty in a very natural way, and she made it seem effortless. If she wore makeup, it wasn't noticeable. That or she was just very good at it? Either way, Jenny had never seen Fiona look unkempt.

"This was exactly what I came in to look for," Fiona admitted. "It's been getting cooler, and I just felt as though I needed a new cardigan to cut the chill. You know how it is. It's too cool for a regular tee but too warm for a sweater. I swear I take them off and put them back on twenty times through the day." She looked at the price and size before nodding. "I think I'll take it."

"Fabulous," Jenny said happily. She turned and walked over to the cash register. "I know exactly what you mean. When I sit down, I get cool, but as soon as I get up and start moving around again, I get warm." She smiled while internally she was debating whether or not she should bring something up that was on her mind. *Just do it*, her mind told her. *You'll regret it if you don't ask her.*

After a few moments, Jenny said, "Don't forget that I still want to see your designs in here someday."

"I know," Fiona sighed. "But I'm not sure that's going to happen. Something's come up." She grimaced apologetically to Jenny.

"What do you mean?" Jenny asked as she rung up the purchase. *Why in the world wouldn't Fiona want to have her designs in my store? Does she have something against me and I don't know it?*

"I've been approached by a clothing line. They're giving my designs a shot, and they're going to put them in all of their stores," Fiona said, barely containing her excitement.

"Oh, wow," Jenny said, but it was hard for her to be happy for Fiona. She'd thought for some time that she and Fiona would eventually be partnering up. To hear that wasn't going to happen was a blow to her self-esteem and what she had planned for the future.

Ever since she'd heard about Fiona's designs and seen some, she'd had that vision in mind. Now it was gone in a puff of smoke, almost as if it had never been there at all. "Good for you," she forced herself to say. She didn't think it was good at all. At least not for her.

"Thank you," Fiona said, oblivious to Jenny's discomfort. "I was really surprised and never expected something like this to happen, but everything just seemed to fall in place.

"Sometimes I swear this is all a dream and someone is going to pinch me at any moment and I'll wake up." She laughed and the sound twisted the knife Jenny felt was lodged in her chest.

The bell over the door rang and a woman she didn't know, but had seen around Cottonwood Springs, entered the shop. She was the pretty blond who worked for the sheriff's department. The woman walked over to the racks against the wall and began to browse, her eyes strictly on the clothing racks.

"If you need any help, please let me know," Jenny told the woman, who nodded in response. She finished the transaction with Fiona and handed her a clothing bag. "Here you go," she said.

"Thanks so much," Fiona said. When she headed for the door, she and the other woman locked eyes and greeted one another. They spoke for a moment but Jenny didn't hear what they were saying. It was probably more talk about Fiona's new venture and Jenny had heard enough about that. Instead, she was frantically wondering how she could have been so wrong about assuming that she and Fiona would be working together. She felt like she'd been completely blindsided.

Just as Fiona was leaving, Jenny's best friend, Ann, walked into the store. Ann visited her at the store from time to time to talk and keep her company. Seeing her bright face and dark blonde hair blowing in the breeze as she walked through the door brought Jenny a bit of peace. At least she could talk to Ann about the situation. Ann had a great perspective on things and could always bring Jenny out of a funk.

"Good afternoon," Ann said after she stepped inside. She glanced over at the woman still browsing, but didn't seem bothered by her presence.

"I'm so glad you're here," Jenny sighed. "Come to the back." She waved her friend around the counter and then turned to her customer. "I'm going to show her a few things in the back. If you need anything while I'm back there, let me know."

The blonde woman nodded and smiled. "Take your time, I'm enjoying doing a little browsing. Do you have a dressing room?" she asked.

Jenny pointed to the bright yellow curtain in the corner. "They're right behind that curtain.

"What's up?" Ann whispered. "You only have me come back here when you need to dish."

"You passed right by Fiona when you walked in," Jenny began. "Well, once again, I tried to get her to put her clothes in my shop."

"And I'll bet she said no because of the clothing company that offered her a deal," Ann said.

"How did you know?" Jenny asked, surprised. "And why didn't you tell me?"

"I'm sorry, but I just found out," Ann apologized. "I was going to tell you today. From what I hear, it's really an amazing opportunity for her. They're going to release her designs and see how they do with them."

"I guess," Jenny sighed. "But I wanted them to be in here."

"There's not much you can do about it now," Ann said with a shrug. "Plus, I guess there's a surprise party in the works to celebrate her success."

"Really?" Jenny asked. "I hadn't heard that."

"It's hush, hush," she said. "They don't want Fiona to find out. I guess the teenage girl Brigid adopted is doing it all. They're getting a cake, they've got the rec room at the church, you know, the whole deal."

"The young girl is giving it for her?" Jenny asked, surprised. "Why does that make me feel worse?"

"I don't know," Ann supplied. Her phone made a noise indicating she had a text. "I have to go. Jeremy's down the street, shopping, and I told him I was just going to run in here for a minute and tell you what I'd heard."

She pulled Jenny into her arms and gave her a tight hug. "It will all work out, you'll see. Don't give up. Your store will still be awesome."

"I'd feel better if her party went up in flames," Jenny grumbled.

"Well, unless you're in the party-crashing business, too, I don't think that's going to happen. It's this weekend. Keep your chin up," she said before hurrying out of the store.

As she left, Jenny followed her to the front of the store and found the woman who was still there standing in front of a full-length mirror. She looked stunning in a mustard yellow wrap dress, her blonde hair tumbling down around her shoulders.

"That looks amazing on you," Jenny said, as she returned her focus to her customer.

"I thought so, too," the woman said, "I'm going to buy it. I have a date tonight and needed something to wear."

"Whoever he is, he's a lucky man," Jenny said, forcing herself to smile.

"Thank you," the woman said as she walked back to the dressing room to change clothes.

Jenny waited for her to come back out, but she couldn't make herself cheer up. She knew it was petty, but she didn't want this party to happen for Fiona. That would make her success real.

To her, it felt as if the party was a signal indicating the start of the demise of her store. She knew it was ridiculous for her to feel that way, but that's how she felt. If she could stop that party from happening, maybe she'd feel a lot better.

"I think I'll take both the dress and this other outfit," the woman said as she walked out of the dressing room.

"Perfect," Jenny said, forcing herself to smile. "Anything you don't want, just put it on the rack and I'll take care of it," she explained. The woman nodded and placed a shirt on the rack, carrying the other clothes to the counter.

"You've got a great selection here in your shop," the woman said. "It's nice to go somewhere that carries real sizes. There's nothing worse than going to the mall and only being able to find the smaller sizes."

"That's exactly why I opened my store," Jenny said. "Just because we aren't supermodels doesn't mean we don't deserve to look nice." She finished ringing up the purchase and before she knew it the woman was walking out the door. Once the door closed, her plastered-on-positivity fell and a look of desperation on her face returned. Now that she was alone, she could think in peace about how she could disrupt the party being given for Fiona.

CHAPTER NINE

"So how are the plans for the party coming along?" Brigid asked Holly as she began to set the table. It had been a long day and Holly was looking forward to sitting down with Brigid and Linc and relaxing. These were Holly's favorite times, when they'd all sit down at the table and eat, the two dogs resting nearby.

"Good, as a matter-of-fact, I have it all taken care of," Holly said as she helped Brigid. It was almost dinner time and Linc was wrapping up the final touches on his shepherd's pie. It was a different recipe from the way he usually prepared it.

"Everything is ordered, I have the key and the room is ready for the decorations to be put up." She'd done everything she could possibly think of to prepare for the party.

"Have you called each place to make sure your orders are going to be ready?" Linc asked as he took the shepherd's pie out of the oven.

"No, should I?" she asked. It never occurred to her to check to make sure the orders would be ready on time. She'd just assumed that they would be. Was that something you were supposed to do?

"It's always a wise thing to do," Brigid said. "Just to make sure they completely understand what you need and when you need it.

Sometimes communications can get tricky, like maybe they forgot to write down your orders, or things have just gotten messed up. It happens," she shrugged. "This way everything is double-checked and you don't have to worry about anything going wrong at the last minute."

As she thought about it, she realized Brigid was right. What better way to make sure everything goes off without a hitch than to confirm everything that was in someone else's hands? These phone calls would certainly put her mind at ease. Then maybe she'd be able to get some sleep without dreaming that something terrible would happen.

"If you don't need me, I'll go do it right now," she said. "I don't want to put it off and end up forgetting." Which was always a possibility with as much as she'd recently had on her mind.

"Sure, go ahead," Brigid nodded. "It shouldn't take you long. Dinner will be ready by the time you get back."

Holly nodded and darted past Jett and Lucky who were lingering around the kitchen, doing their best to look sad and hungry so hopefully, Linc would take pity on them, and they could have a bite of shepherd's pie.

When she got to her room, Holly sat down at her computer and brought up the phone number for the bakery first. She pressed in the numbers on her phone and leaned back in her chair. But when the person on the other end answered and she began to inquire about her order, a chill ran through her.

"What do you mean it was canceled?" Holly asked.

"A woman called in saying she didn't need the cake anymore and that the party had been canceled," the young woman on the other end of the line said. "The person said their name was Holly Lewis, knew the date of the party, and everything. It never occurred to me to question it," she admitted. "Are you telling me it wasn't you?"

"No," Holly said quickly, "it wasn't."

"Oh, I'm so sorry," she said. "Don't worry about it. I'll add it back to the order list, but it's a good thing you called to check on your order. We still have time to make it. Nothing's changed, right?" she asked.

"No, nothing's changed," Holly said, her mind reeling. "Thank you."

"It's no problem," she said. "And I'll even give you a little bonus for your trouble. I should have made sure it was you. Someone must have it in for you."

Holly insisted she didn't have to, but the young woman insisted. She kept telling Holly how sorry she was, but how was she to know that it wasn't Holly? By the time she ended the call, Holly felt slightly better.

"Wow," she said to herself. "That could have been bad. I guess I better call the deli too," she decided. If someone had tried to cancel her cake order, there was a good chance they might try at other places, too.

She looked up the number and punched it in.

"Willard's deli," the man on the other end said.

"Hi, this is Holly Lewis. I just wanted to confirm my platters for the party I'm having this weekend." She did her best to keep her voice strong and firm, even though she was quivering inside. She stood up from her desk and began to pace.

"Hi, Holly," the man said. "Let me look over our orders." He paused and made a little noise while he searched. "Nope, I see that it was canceled."

"Seriously?" she asked, exasperated. *How could this be happening?* she wondered. *And why was someone doing this? It didn't make any sense.*

She dropped down, sitting on the edge of her bed.

"You didn't call in to cancel the order?" the man asked. He was clearly as surprised as the young woman from the bakery had been.

"No," she said, feeling tears starting to form. "Someone called the bakery too, and canceled my order over there." Her voice wavered, but she couldn't help it.

"Oh, I see," he said. "Well, it's not a problem. I still have your order ticket here on the desk. I'll just put a note on it that it wasn't canceled and make sure it's prepared. You said someone called the bakery, too?" he asked.

"Yes," Holly said, her voice thick with emotion. She wanted to burst into tears, but knew she couldn't, anyway not yet.
"Don't worry. I'll make it myself and the only way you can cancel this time is if you come in personally and tell me," he said, full of compassion. "I don't see why someone would do something like that. It's never happened before."

The door to her room squeaked open and she saw Jett pushing on her bedroom door. Lucky wasn't far behind him.

"I'm so sorry for the trouble this causes you," she said, trying her best to not sound as emotional as she felt. Jett walked right up to her and laid his massive head on her leg. She caressed his soft face and his eyes closed as Lucky jumped up on the bed and sat down next to her.

"No, don't be. You don't have anything to apologize for," he said. "But if I were you, I sure would want to find out who did this and almost threw a monkey wrench in your party plans. I'm so glad you called to confirm."

Holly nodded and then realized he couldn't see her. "Me too, thank you so much," she said before hanging up. Tossing her phone on her bed, she allowed a few tears to slip down her cheeks. She looked down at Jett and Lucky who were both looking up at her with compassion in their eyes.

"Why would someone do this?" she asked them quietly. Who would want to ruin the party enough that they'd call and cancel her orders? She was heartbroken and worried. What if there was something else going on? Was there someone out there trying to make her look bad again? It had happened before when she'd created the website for Linc and Brigid's B & B.

Could someone else be out to get her? But then she began to wonder if it was really about her, or if it was actually about Fiona. Perhaps someone didn't want a party being given for Fiona?

"Well, they didn't succeed," she told the dogs. "Thankfully, I was able to undo their damage." Wiping her face, she stood up and headed back to the kitchen. She needed to tell Brigid and Linc what she'd found out.

"Everything in order?" Linc asked as she returned. He'd just finished scooping out the shepherd's pie onto their dinner plates.

"Kind of," she said softly. The way her voice broke made them both look up.

"What's wrong?" Brigid asked as she froze. All it took was a glance at Holly's tear-stained face to clue her in that something wasn't right.

Holly slowly walked over to the table and sat down. Lucky jumped up in her lap, and Jett sat down next to her. She hadn't realized they'd followed her from her room. "Someone called the deli and bakery and canceled my orders."

"What?" Brigid and Linc said at the same time. "Who would do that?" Linc asked as he turned to Brigid.

"Did you tell them it wasn't you?" Brigid asked. She was poised on her seat, as if she were ready to spring into action. Knowing her, she probably was.

"I did," Holly nodded. "And they both said it would still be ready for me on time, but I'm more worried about who did it. Why would someone want to sabotage my party for Fiona?"

"I don't know," Brigid murmured. "But it's a good thing you called. You cut them off at the pass, and your party is still on. You have all your decorations and things, right?" she asked as she looked closely at Holly.

Holly nodded. "They're in my room." She was so glad she hadn't put them somewhere else. She'd have had trouble replacing everything she'd gotten, given the fact there were so many balloons, streamers, and confetti.

"Then it seems to me the crisis has been averted," Brigid said, relaxing somewhat. "But that still seems odd. Maybe we should look into it?" It was apparent that Brigid's gears were starting to turn as she caught a whiff of a possible investigation case.

Holly thought about it for a moment and then shook her head. "No. I don't want to start something. Besides, whoever did it probably doesn't know that their plan was stopped. If we go poking around, they may figure it out and do something else to stop the party. Let's just go on like nothing happened," she said.

"Are you sure?" Brigid asked. "You still have two days before the party. What if they try something else?" Holly could see her point, but she didn't want to think that way.

"It'll be fine," Holly sighed. "I don't see how else they could mess it up. Maybe we'll try to figure it out afterwards, but for now, I have enough on my plate to deal with."

And it was true. There was a lot going on at school and Fiona had been giving her more responsibilities at the bookstore. It wasn't that she didn't enjoy the extra workload, and learning about the financials of the business was actually fascinating.

"If something else crops up, we'll look into it and see what we can do about it. Until then, I'm not going to give it a second thought."

"If that's what you want to do," Brigid conceded. "I just hope for their sake they don't try anything else. "Otherwise they are going to have a lot of angry people on their hands."

"You're lucky you found out now," Linc said. "Can you imagine how upset the guests would be at going to a party where there was no food?"

"I think they were trying to make it look like I didn't know what I was doing," Holly said. "I'll bet they were banking on the fact that I'm young and probably wouldn't double-check the orders. After all, if you hadn't said anything about it, Brigid, I never would have thought to confirm them."

"That tells you it's probably not someone your age," Brigid said as she raised one finger. "It also tells me that it's someone old enough to have thrown a party or two."

"You're starting to investigate," Linc said in a sing-song voice.

"Sorry," Brigid said, looking chastised. "Can't help it. It's a habit."

"I know it is," Linc chuckled as he reached for her hand. "I just like to give you some trouble when you do it."

"Let's just cross our fingers and pray this is the end of it," Holly sighed. "Because I don't want to lose any more sleep over this."

"You'll see, it will all work out," Brigid said confidently.

CHAPTER TEN

"I really appreciate you guys coming to help me decorate," Holly said as she unlocked the rec room at the church. She'd met Wade and Levi in the parking lot of the church, so they could help her decorate the room.

Originally, she'd planned on doing it all herself, but then she thought better of it. It would be boring to do it all alone, but if she had some company the time would pass a lot faster, plus she'd get a lot more done.

"I wasn't sure I'd be able to do it all myself." She pushed the door open and Wade held it for her as she walked inside.

"You know I'm always up for decorating," Levi grinned. "I love a good party, so I can't help but think that decorating for one would be fun too."

"And you know I'll help you, no matter what," Wade said as he took her hand. His thumb landed on her promise ring, and he wiggled it a little to remind her it was there. She felt a blush rise in her cheeks.

"I know," she said while she flipped on the lights. She set down the bags that held the streamers and decorations. She'd brought everything else in earlier in the day and this was the last of it. "I still need to get the deli trays out of my car, but if you two can start lining the tables up in two rows with one at the front, we can get started."

Levi and Wade nodded and started to work as she returned to her car. On the way over she'd stopped to pick up the food, knowing there was a kitchen area with a refrigerator. She'd already spoken to Brigid about getting the cake tomorrow. Her plan was to have everything already set up and then Brigid just had to unlock the room, bring in the cake and let in the guests who were set to show up at 5:30.

Meanwhile, Holly would keep Fiona preoccupied at work until Abra came in for her shift that evening. Abra only had to work a couple of hours, so she'd be able to come to the party later, but she was okay with that. Someone needed to handle the store and not tip Fiona off. Abra had been happy to do it and made Holly promise to record the whole thing for her so she could see Fiona's face when she walked through the door.

When Holly returned with the last of the trays, she was glad to see that Wade and Levi had set up the tables exactly where she wanted them. The room was already starting to take shape.

"Now what do you want us to do?" Levi asked.

Holly began to open the bags of decorations they'd carried in and started laying it all out on the tables. "Let's do the tablecloths first," she decided as she looked at everything. "They need to be on the tables before anything else can go on them, so we should probably start there.

"I have several different ones, because I was going for a colorful look. As long as we don't have two tables next to each other that are the same color, we should be good." She tore open the plastic wrapper and started to unfold one. Levi and Wade followed suit, and soon they were hard at work laying out tablecloths.

"Hey, I have a little stereo out in my car," Wade volunteered. "Why don't I go get it so we can have something to listen to while we work?"

"Great idea!" Holly said. "That'll make this all go much quicker." Music always seemed to make any chore she had to do more enjoyable. There was no reason this wouldn't be the same.

While Wade was going to his car, Levi slipped over to stand closer to Holly. "I saw the ring on your finger," he muttered conspiratorially.

"Oh?" Holly said with a little smile.

"I did," Levi said. "And I noticed the finger it's on. Do you have something you need to share with your best friend?" he asked as he wiggled his eyebrows at her.

"It's just a promise ring," Holly said as she showed him. "We're not engaged or anything. It's like an engagement to be engaged," she explained. She still thought it was crazy to even think about that being part of her future, but at the same time she couldn't imagine ever loving someone else the way she loved Wade.

"That's so cute," Levi said as he shook his head. "A promise to each other that you'll get engaged. You two are like an old couple in teenage bodies."

"Is there something wrong with that?" she asked. She kind of liked how her relationship with Wade was. While other couples their age were being dramatic, breaking up only to get back together, she and Wade had promised each other to not assume anything and to ask direct questions to one another.

So far it seemed to be working. They hardly ever fought, and if one of them hurt the other's feelings for whatever reason, they talked about it and worked it out. No bottling things up only to have them explode later. They'd seen enough of their friends do that to know it wasn't the answer.

"No," Levi said. "It's just not normal teenage behavior. You two should be partying and stuff, not knitting sweaters and drinking the morning coffee together. Do you guys look over the classified ads and consider going to auctions together?"

Holly let out a loud burst of laughter. "We don't do that!"

Levi grinned. "Well, you practically do," he teased. "I'm telling you that you two are aging before your time. It's such a waste." He tsked, but then he smiled to let her know he was only kidding. "But I wouldn't have you two act any other way. At this point, if you started acting like teenagers, I'd be worried."

The door opened and Wade walked in. "Here we go," he said as he set the small Bluetooth speaker on a table. "Do you have any requests? I can search for whatever you're in the mood for if I don't have it."

"Just something upbeat," Levi said as he started digging through the rest of the bags of decorations. "I want something that will get me dancing. That will liven this place up a bit. We can get the party started the day before." He gave Holly a sly grin and she shook her head. "Oh, these are cute," he said as he held up one of the model sketches that Holly had glued to a stick.

"Those are actually some of Fiona's sketches. I enlarged them and then printed them on cardstock before cutting them out. This way, guests can see some of her handiwork," Holly said proudly.

"That's a great idea," Wade said as he started the music and then turned back towards them. He pulled another one out of the bag and held it up. "So Fiona drew this?"

"She did," Holly nodded. "I just picked some of my favorites."

"What exactly are you going to do with these?" Levi asked.

"Here, let me show you," she said. She walked over to the corner of the room, picked up a box she'd dropped off earlier, and carried it to the table. "There are vases in here," she said as she pulled open the top. "We'll stick one of these in first," she demonstrated. "Then we'll get these glittery spray looking things and stick them in too.

"Then I thought we'd pour some of these stones in to hide the sticks. I don't know if we'd be able to get them in if we put the stones in first." She made one up to show them. "There, see?" she said as she held it up.

Wade looked around at the tables which all had tablecloths. "And we need one for each table?" he asked.

"That's the plan. I hope I have enough," Holly said as she tapped her fingers on her chin.

"It looks like you do," Levi said as he unpacked more supplies. "But we won't know until we start assembling them."

Together they started building the centerpieces while laughing and joking with each other. Before long, Levi was singing to the music and being silly while Wade and Holly laughed and enjoyed the show.

After they'd worked for a while, Levi's phone began to ring. "Quiet. It's my mom," he said right before he answered. He walked away from the music, heading to a far corner while Wade turned the volume down. By then they'd hung the streamers, gotten all of the centerpieces in place, and were almost done with the main decorating. They finished filling the balloons with helium and tying them to the weights so they could be placed in the corners.

"This is really looking great," Wade said quietly, trying to not disturb Levi.

"Thanks," Holly said proudly. "It's actually turning out way better than I thought it would."

"I've got to go home, guys," Levi said as he walked back to them. "Mom is headed this way to pick me up."

"Thank you so much for helping me," Holly said as she pulled him in for a hug. "I really appreciate it."

"It's no trouble," he said as he squeezed her back. "That's what friends are for. Send me a picture when you're all done. I want to see it before anyone else does."

Holly promised and Levi gave them a wave before heading outside to wait for his mother.

"This is going to be a great party," Wade said as he started adding confetti to each table.

"I sure hope so," Holly said.

CHAPTER ELEVEN

Holly hadn't realized just how hard it was going to be to keep Fiona's party a secret from her. Especially since now it was the big day and she was working side by side with her. How could she not accidentally slip and say something about the party while she was right there?

She couldn't wait to see Fiona's face when she walked into the room. Holly had hardly slept the night before because she'd been so excited. Seeing the room completely decorated and ready for the party had made the whole thing much more real. It was no longer just an idea, but something that was actually going to happen.

As she sat behind the register, Holly began to imagine what it would be like when she was able to watch Fiona walk through the door and realize that the party was just for her. Holly had already worked it out with Fiona's husband, Brandon, that he'd drive her and their son, little Aiden, to the party.

Holly was so glad she wouldn't be the one driving Fiona to the party, because she wasn't sure she'd have been able to keep from spilling the beans. She continued to envision the party and the shocked look on Fiona's face as she rung up customers and wished them a great day.

"Earth to Holly. Come in, Holly," she heard Fiona say from

behind her. Startled, she turned around.

"Yeah?" she said quickly. She hadn't realized Fiona was trying to get her attention.

"What's gotten into you today?" Fiona asked, her brow wrinkled in concern. "You seem to be somewhere else. Are you getting sick or something?" She studied Holly closely, as if she might be able to read what was wrong on her skin. Or maybe she was trying to evaluate if she had something contagious.

"I'm sorry," Holly said as she stood up from her chair and stretched. She needed an excuse and fast. Something simple yet believable. "I didn't get a whole lot of sleep last night. I'm kind of zapped."

There was no way she could admit she was spacing out while she thought about the surprise party that was going to take place in a few hours. Besides, it wasn't a complete lie. She really was tired. Tired of holding in her secret. The day couldn't go by fast enough for Holly.

"Do you need to go home?" Fiona asked. She looked concerned, which made Holly feel kind of bad. "Feel free to take off and get some rest. I can handle things on my own. I used to do it all the time, remember? I don't want anything bogging down my best employee. Trust me, I can manage." She leaned against the doorway that led to the back room.

"No, I think I'm okay," Holly said as she looked up at her. She just needed to focus on work and not on what was going to happen later, then she'd be fine. "Maybe I just need to move around a little." She started twisting a little to make her point. "You know, get the blood pumping and wake me up."

"If you're sure," Fiona said, still eyeing her suspiciously. "I'll be back here entering the new books into the system. Let me know if you change your mind. I get it that you've got a lot going on at school. Brigid told me you'd been busy planning some project. Just try not to fall asleep on me, okay?" She didn't seem entirely convinced, but she was clearly taking Holly at her word.

"No problem," Holly said, nodding. "I think I'll vacuum out here while we don't have anyone browsing. Those leaves that keep blowing in are making a mess of the carpet." Anything to put a little distance between her and Fiona so she wouldn't accidentally say something she didn't want to.

Fiona looked around and nodded. "Yeah, that's probably a good idea. I've been thinking about doing it myself, but just haven't managed to do it today. Knock yourself out," she said before heading back to what she was doing.

Holly sighed in relief. She really needed to get it together. Fiona was a smart woman. If she kept this up, she'd figure out that something was going on. Better to put a little distance between them, rather than ruin the surprise.

Dragging out the vacuum from its place in the back, she wheeled it out to the front room and plugged it in. She pushed it over closer to the door, where the main concentration of leaf debris was. She caught a glimpse of the time and realized that Brigid was probably picking up the cake and taking it to the rec room right then.

Holly had told Brigid the night before that she was really happy with how the decorations had turned out, and Brigid had said she was eager to see them. Any moment now, Holly was looking forward to a text from Brigid telling her what she thought. Hopefully, she'd think they were great too. Pushing the power button with her foot, she began to vacuum.

Sucking up each leaf, she started to wonder if she'd invited everyone she should have. Holly was sure that it was just party jitters making her think she may have missed someone. Still, she mentally went over the guest list in her mind to try to soothe her nerves and solidify in her mind that she hadn't missed anyone.

As she finished vacuuming, her cell phone began to ring in her back pocket. Checking it, she saw it was Brigid. *I bet she wants to tell me how great the room looks,* Holly thought as she answered. *Although I was kind of expecting a text instead of a call. Hopefully I can make it not too obvious what we're talking about.*

"Do you like it?" Holly asked quietly, trying to not let Fiona overhear her conversation. Hopefully she was deep into whatever she was doing and not paying any attention.

"Holly," Brigid began, her voice low and calm. "We have a problem." With those four words, Holly felt her heart fall into her stomach. She'd been worried about this ever since she'd started planning the party.

"What is it?" she asked all the while thinking *please let it just be the cake. Please, please, please, just be the cake. A cake was easily fixed. If anything, the bakery could always redo the icing.*

"Something has happened to all of your decorations. It's hard to explain. Tell Fiona whatever you need to tell her so you can leave. You should be here." Her voice sounded grim, making Holly even more nervous. Very rarely did Brigid get dark like that. It had to be something serious.

"Um, okay," she said. "I'll be there in a minute," she promised before she ended the call.

Her mind began to race and she tried to tell herself that everything was going to be okay, but it was hard to convince herself of that after Brigid's cryptic words. She had to get to the church so that she could see what had happened. That was the only way she was going to be able to get through this.

Her mind was creating the worst-case scenarios, and it wasn't helping her to remain calm. She had to go evaluate the damage and make a plan to fix it. She could still pull this off. She had to.

Wrapping the cord back up around the vacuum, she did her best to look tired as she returned to the back room. She even yawned loudly for an added effect.

"Hey, Fiona," she began as she put the vacuum back where it was kept. She allowed her shoulders to slump, so that she looked defeated.

"What's up?" Fiona asked as she turned around to look at Holly.

"I think you're right," Holly began. "I'm just too tired to function today. I think a nap is exactly what I need right now. I don't want to mess anything up from being so tired." She did her best to appear sleepy, even though now she was anything but. "I wanted to sort books, but I don't think I'd do a very good job at this point."

"No problem, kiddo," Fiona said as she stood up and crossed the room. She wrapped her arms around Holly and hugged her. "Trust me, I completely understand. I have a toddler at home, and I bet I've felt like that a few hundred times by now. Go get some rest. This will all still be waiting for you when you're better rested." She gave her a kiss on the forehead and told her she'd see her later as Holly headed to her car.

Knowing something bad had happened to the decorations made her afraid to go see what had happened. Still, she was hopeful with maybe a few changes, they could still pull off the party. She didn't have any more money to replace anything, but maybe they could do something with the decorations. As she started driving towards the church, she crossed her fingers and prayed it would all be okay.

When she pulled into the parking lot and saw Brigid waiting for her, a thread of fear shot through her. It had to be bad if Brigid wanted to prepare her first. As she climbed out of her car, Brigid hurried over.

"Jordan is calling Missy right now," she said quickly as if that were Holly's main concern right now. "And I have a plan. No matter how bad it looks, just know I have a plan." The way she was insisting Holly know this before even seeing the damage made her even more worried. Her hands began to tremble.

"You're kind of freaking me out right now, Brigid," Holly

admitted. "Is it really that bad?" She searched Brigid's face, hoping for some sort of hint. Something that said this could even be a joke. But she found no trace of that. Only worry and determination.

"I'll let you be the judge of that," Brigid said as she took Holly's hand. As they walked together, Holly felt as if they were walking in slow motion. Each step was so agonizingly slow, it was almost painful. Part of her wanted to break free and bolt for the door so she could see what had happened. Almost like ripping off a band-aid, she wanted to get this over with.

When they finally made it to the door, Brigid put her hand on the knob. "Are you ready?" she asked.

Holly wanted to scream for her to just open the door, but instead, she just nodded. "I'm ready."

Brigid opened the door and let Holly step inside.

The first thing she noticed was the streamers. Her eyes began at the ceiling, noticing the sad remnants of color that still clung to the top of the room. As her eyes traveled downward, she saw the stripped tables and all her decorations on the floor. Her heart started beating faster as she looked at the corners for her balloon bouquets but they were all popped and ruined. Nothing had been left untouched. Tables had been overturned, streamers shredded, pillows in a mess on the floor, and everything scattered as if the wind had been angry.

Tears began to form as she looked around. "I locked the room," she said softly. "I know I did because I double-checked just to be sure. How could this happen?"

Even as she stood there looking at the disaster, she replayed the memory of her locking the door in her mind over and over again, just to make sure she'd done it right. She remembered she'd even pushed on the door to make sure it was locked.

"The room was locked," Brigid nodded. "I had to use the key to get in, and I found it this way." Brigid walked farther into the room. "I came in, set the cake down on this table and went looking for Missy," she began.

"I guess she'd just left to go to the store, so instead I found Jordan. I showed him what happened, and he hurried to call Missy so we can get to the bottom of this."

"Missy's not here?" Holly asked, only half hearing Brigid. She was too distracted by the devastation around them.

"No, but she will be soon," Brigid promised as she put her arm around Holly. "Unfortunately, this isn't all of it. But I want you to know I'm working on fixing it. Just keep that in mind, okay?"

Holly nodded as tears ran down her cheeks. The feeling almost surprised her because she hadn't realized she'd felt like crying. "What else is there?" she asked. Brigid kept her arm around Holly's shoulders as she led her to the little kitchen area. "No, no, no, no," Holly began repeating. "Please tell me they didn't mess up the food too. Please, not the food."

Brigid pushed open the door and led Holly inside. She didn't want to look. She wasn't sure she could take seeing any more devastation, but she found herself looking anyway, like a car accident you couldn't turn away from. The floor was almost completely covered with food, paper plates, napkins, and even the plasticware. Whoever had done this wanted to make sure nothing would be usable. "I'm just glad the cake wasn't here," Brigid said as she opened the fridge and showed Holly.

The cake looked beautiful and just as she imagined. They'd decorated the edges to have balloons, streamers and confetti while writing "Way to go, Fiona!" along the length of it. At this point, it was the only thing left of the party.

"How could this happen?" Holly asked, starting to breathe heavily. It was suddenly incredibly hot in the kitchen. She began pulling at her collar. "I don't understand. I locked the door. How-

Why- I just-" she stuttered before finally breaking down in sobs.

"Come on," Brigid said gently. "Let's get you outside for some fresh air." She led Holly out of the kitchen and across the rec room.

"I have to call Wade," Holly began. "I have to tell him what's happened."

"You can, sweetie," Brigid said softly, doing her best to console her. "But let's get out of here first, okay?"

Holly nodded and allowed Brigid to lead her out of the building. She couldn't look at the mess anymore. The senseless waste was sickening and for what? Why would someone want to destroy a party? It didn't make any sense at all to her. Only someone cold and with no heart would do something like this to someone. That was the only explanation for it.

CHAPTER TWELVE

"There's Jordan," Brigid said as she and Holly stood outside the church. "Are you going to be okay while I go talk to him?" She ducked down low so that she could make eye contact with Holly, whose eyes were fixed on the ground. She didn't want to look at anyone. What she really wanted was for someone to pinch her and wake her up from this nightmare.

Holly nodded her head. "Yeah, go ahead," she muttered as she sniffled. Anyway, she wasn't exactly good company right now. All she felt like doing was standing there and feeling sorry for herself. That's when she remembered that she still hadn't called Wade. Once Brigid had walked far enough away, Holly pulled out her phone and dialed Wade's number.

"Holly, you never call me," he said as he answered. "What's going on?"

She sniffled again, tears still streaming down her face. "Someone destroyed the party. The decorations, the food, everything," she said, her voice thick with tears. "But I locked the door. I swear it. I locked the door, but they still got in."

"I'll be right there," he promised. "Don't go anywhere."

They ended the call and Holly swiped at her eyes. Sure, Brigid said she'd take care of it, but how could she fix this? How could she replace the food, the decorations, and everything before all of the guests showed up? It seemed like an impossible task, especially for one teenager who'd spent her money on everything that had been destroyed. All she could think about was how it was all for nothing. Wasted.

How could this happen? She was sure she'd locked the rec room door. So how could someone get into a locked room? She wanted to just stay where she was, leaning against the outside of the building, and feel sorry for herself, but suddenly a thought came to her. Whoever had done this had to be the same person who had canceled her orders.

That was a clue that led to another mystery for her to solve. Someone had managed to get into a locked room in order to destroy everything. As she started thinking about other possible clues, her tears began to dry. That's what she needed to focus on. Not the destruction, but instead, focusing on finding out how this happened.

She couldn't stand around crying and feeling sorry for herself. No, she needed to figure out who did this. Doing something like this had to be a crime. Destroying someone else's property had to be illegal. But at the same time, financially it really wasn't a lot. Would the sheriff's department even be interested enough to look into it?

"Holly, I'm so sorry," Jordan began as he walked up to her. He and Brigid had finished talking, and he'd hurried over. Looking up at him, Holly could see the sadness in his eyes. "Missy's on her way now. We'll get to the bottom of this. Someone else had to have a key."

"Exactly," Brigid said, nodding. "Plus, we can salvage some of the decorations. Things like confetti and tablecloths aren't that expensive to replace, anyway. Don't worry about the food. We'll get that figured out. The cake is safe, so we're halfway there. It looks worse than it is. We just need a team to clean up the mess and start putting it all back together." She rubbed her hand up and down Holly's arm, trying to make her feel better.

"I have to figure out who did this," Holly began. "They can't get away with it." She was frustrated beyond belief and needed something to put her energy into.

"They won't," Brigid reassured her. "Whoever it was did not have permission to be in the rec room. Jordan and I were talking about it before you got here. They had to have gotten a key in order to get in there, but they still didn't have permission to be in there. Plus, they destroyed property. There are legal repercussions for that sort of thing."

"She's right," Jordan said, nodding. "And we will press charges. But for now, I'm going to help Brigid make this right for you. Whatever needs to be done, it's going to be taken care of. If you can discover who did this, then that's even better."

A car approached and they turned to see if it was Missy. Instead, they saw Wade pull up with Levi in the passenger seat. Holly couldn't believe it. She hadn't said anything about Levi, but seeing his face and brightly colored hair made her feel slightly better. His face was full of concern, so she knew Wade had filled him in on the way over.

"I figured you'd need lots of help," Wade explained as he climbed out of his car. "I called Levi and told him what was going on. He wanted to come and do what he could to make things right for the party."

"You guys," Holly said as she rushed towards them, hugging each of them in turn. "Thank you," she whispered to Wade as she kissed him. "Go in and look at it," she told them.

"I can't stand to go in and see it again, but you might as well see what we're up against. They trashed the kitchen too, so don't forget to look in there. I want you to get the full effect." She couldn't help but sound a little bitter about it, but she felt she had every right to be at that moment.

Wade and Levi headed into the rec room, leaving Holly, Brigid, and Jordan outside. "Looks like we're building a good clean-up crew," Brigid said confidently. "We should probably get pictures."

"I'll take them," Jordan said as he pulled out his phone.

While they were discussing what should be documented, Missy drove up. Holly noticed that there were bags in the backseat, but Missy completely ignored them and rushed to Holly's side.

"I can't believe this happened," she said quickly. "Is everything a loss? I promise, Holly, this won't stop your party. I feel personally responsible. This never should have happened."

"I think it's easiest if you just take a look yourself," Holly sighed. "I'd rather not think about it at the moment."

"Come, I'll show you," Jordan said as he took his wife by the hand and led her to the door. "I need to take pictures anyway."

Brigid leaned up against the side of the building with Holly. "Do you have any idea who may have done this?" she asked after Missy and Jordan had gone inside.

Holly shook her head. "No, not that I can think of. I mean, who would destroy a party? Doesn't everyone like a good party? And it doesn't just affect me or Fiona. It's like they were trying to take the party away from everyone. Who would do such a thing?"

She'd been struggling with that thought ever since she'd seen how bad it was, because it wasn't like they were just trying to mess it up a little. Whoever had done it had been dead set on making sure they ruined absolutely everything they could.

"That's what we need to figure out," Brigid said. "Now's the time to think logically. You know how this works. We have to collect clues, think of suspects, and narrow them down one by one. I called Linc, but he's busy with the guests at the B & B.

"I called the sheriff and told him that we don't have any suspects as yet. He's out of town at the moment, so he said if we need any information to contact Deputy Keegan, and she'd help us." She bumped Holly's shoulder with her own. "We've figured out tougher cases than this. We'll find out who did this."

Holly nodded. "I don't have any more money to replace the decorations," she said as she looked up. She'd already tried to figure out how she could buy more and knew she simply couldn't.

"I told you, don't worry about this," Brigid repeated, waving her hand. "You figure out who did this, and I'll take care of the rest. I promise I'll have it ready in time."

"Are you sure?" Holly asked, uncertain. "I can always call everyone and cancel it."

"I'm positive," Brigid assured her. "Whoever did this is not going to win. They wanted to stop this party, so I'm going to do everything I can to make sure the party goes on. We don't back down to bullies around here, and that's exactly what this person is, a cowardly bully."

Wade and Missy returned from the room, heads hung low. They didn't speak until they were back by Holly's side.

"Holly, I don't know what to say," Missy began. "I feel like this is my fault." Her eyes were wide and pleading.

"How could it be your fault?" Holly asked. "You didn't do this. You couldn't have predicted this would happen."

"No, I didn't," Missy said. "But I'm the one with the keys. Jordan told me that the room was locked. That means someone had to get one of my spare keys so they could get in. That's on me." Missy's eyes began to water. "I'm so very sorry."

"Don't beat yourself up, Missy," Holly said as she lightly touched her arm. Missy's tears began to slip down her face. "How could you know that someone would do something like this? You're a trusting person and someone took advantage of that trust."

"I should have paid more attention," she said as she wiped her face. "Jordan and Levi are seeing what they can save now."

"I'm going to go help," Brigid said. "Are you going to be okay?" she asked Holly.

Holly nodded. "I will be."

"Good, now get started figuring out who did this. Remember, if you need any information, call Deputy Keegan," she reminded her.

"I will," Holly promised. After Brigid went inside, she turned to Missy. "We're going to have to think of anyone who might want to destroy everything and had access to the keys."

Wade pulled out his phone. "I'll make a list in my notes. Who do you know that could have gotten the keys?"

Missy led them around the corner to a bench and they sat down. "I've been asking myself the same thing ever since Jordan called and told me what happened," she admitted. "And the only person I can think of is Jada."

"Who's Jada?" Wade asked.

"She's my niece who's here visiting from Baltimore. I overheard her talking about the party to someone on her phone the other day. She seemed a little catty about it, but I didn't think anything of it at the time because honestly, she's been that way almost from the moment she got here," Missy explained.

"But why would she want to mess up Holly's party?" he asked.

Missy shrugged. "I have no clue, but she's the first person who came to mind when I started to think of who would have had access to the keys. I don't want to assume anything, but I'm not sure who else would. I mean, I have people in the church all the time, but not many actually go into my office."

"We'll have to see what she was doing last night. We left around 9:00, so whoever did this did it sometime after that," Holly pointed out. That's when she remembered something. "Do you know someone named Jodi who recently moved back to Cottonwood Springs? She used to be Fiona's friend. I can't remember her last name."

"Jodi Young?" Missy asked. "She came by to visit me the other day."

"Really?" Holly asked. "That's interesting."

"Why?" Wade asked, trying to follow the conversation.

"Brigid and I ran into her at the store the other day. We told her about the party and Fiona's success, and she didn't seem all that happy about it." As Holly explained it, the fact that she'd visited Missy seemed somewhat suspicious. Could she have come to the church just to scope out where the party was going to be held?

"Well, first things first, let's go talk to Jada," Missy said as she stood up. "I don't want to think she did it, but I won't be able to get what I heard out of my head until I hear from her."

"Right behind you," Holly said as they stood up and followed her.

CHAPTER THIRTEEN

Wade and Holly followed Missy around the church to her home in the back. It almost appeared to be a separate building, but there was actually a hallway that led to it from the church. They circled around to the front door and waited for Missy to open it.

As they walked in through the front door, Missy turned to Holly and said, "She's probably in her room, which is our guest room. I'll go get her."

Holly nodded. "Okay, sounds good."

"Go ahead and make yourselves comfortable, I'll be right back." Missy turned and hurried towards the hallway.

The room was cozy with a large area rug in the center and a couple of couches facing the TV. A fireplace was in the corner and a beautiful china cabinet took up one of the walls. There was a dining room through a large archway and a kitchen beyond that. She and Wade sat next to each other on one of the couches, waiting for Missy to return.

"What's this girl like?" Wade asked as they waited. "Does she seem like the type of person who'd want to destroy a complete stranger's party?"

"She's not the friendliest person I've ever met," Holly admitted. "I guess her parents are having a tough time, and she came to stay with Missy and Jordan while they try to work things out."

"Tough break," Wade sighed. "I'm sure that's been pretty hard on her. Do you think it's possible she did this?"

Holly shrugged. "I mean, she's right here, so she could have, but what would be her motive? I don't really see why she'd even want to do something like that. I guess she could just be one of those people who like to destroy things, but I didn't get that kind of vibe from her the other day."

She struggled to recall everything that was said when she'd come to look at the room, but couldn't think of anything that would give an indication the girl didn't like her. But then again, Missy did say that she'd overhead Jada talking about Holly on the phone. Maybe she'd misread the situation. Maybe Jada was one of those girls who looked down her nose at people and just acted like a jerk in general.

"Can't you just tell me what's going on?" she heard Jada say as her voice grew louder. "I was right in the middle of a good episode."

"Please, I need you to answer a few questions," Missy said. "Don't make this difficult. It's a simple request." They heard a door being slammed and then stomping that sounded as though it was coming their way.

"She sounds delightful," Wade muttered. Holly felt herself tense up in anticipation of Jada coming. Now that she was angry for having to walk away from whatever she was watching, Holly hoped she'd be somewhat cooperative, but the tone that had been in her voice when she was yelling at Missy didn't sound too promising.

When Jada came into view, she stopped when she saw Holly sitting on the couch. If looks could kill, Holly was fairly certain she'd be dead. "What do you want?" Jada asked, crossing her arms.

"Please, take a seat," Missy said, urging her into the living room.

Jada sighed while she rolled her eyes and heavily walked over to the nearest seat before flopping down. She was doing everything she could to let them know she didn't want to be there.

"Holly decorated the rec room last night," Missy began. "But during the night, someone went in and ruined all of her decorations along with the things in the kitchen. Is there anything you can tell us about that?"

"You think I did it?" Jada asked as she glared at Holly, her eyes looking like daggers. "Wow." She flopped back against the couch.

"I didn't say that," Holly said, speaking up. "We're just trying to figure out who could have done it. The door was locked, so whoever did it had access to the keys. I'm not trying to throw blame anywhere. We're just starting from the beginning."

"The only people who have access to those keys are Jordan, you, and me," Missy explained. "Since I know it wasn't either one of us, you were the next one on the list. We just want to know if you know anything about it. Nobody said you did anything."

"Well I don't know anything, okay?" Jada huffed. She kicked her foot out and began to rub the toe of her boot along the edge of the coffee table. "I did see her go in late last night to decorate, though," she said, nodding towards Holly. Jada turned towards her, "I thought it was weird you didn't turn the lights on. How did you decorate in the dark?"

Holly shook her head. "I didn't. And I didn't go alone. Wade and Levi were with me." She turned to look at Wade and then turned back to Jada. "Can you describe this person?" If Jada had seen someone go into the building, maybe she'd be able to identify them. She might not live around here, but that didn't mean they couldn't get pictures and have her pick the person out from there.

Jada shook her head. "No. And honestly, I just assumed it was you. I knew you had a key, so I didn't pay too much attention. I watched them unlock the door and then go inside."

"What were you doing where you could see all of this?" Missy asked.

Jada looked down and picked at her peeling black nail polish. "I needed some air."

Missy nodded, seeming to understand what that meant and lowered her voice. "You spoke to your parents again, didn't you?" she asked.

Jada nodded, fighting back tears. "I told them I wanted to come home, but they told me I couldn't. Not yet. But I just want to go home."

"I'm sorry," Holly said gently. "It must be hard being halfway across the country from home and not knowing anyone." She remembered how odd it was for her when she visited her aunt, uncle, and cousins in Springfield, Missouri.

Jada nodded and angrily swiped at her eyes. "I just want to get back to my friends. I hate this place."

"It's really not so bad here," Wade volunteered. He'd silently been watching the exchange, and seemed moved by Jada's predicament. "Maybe you can come and hang out with us sometime. It would at least give you something to do," he suggested.

"Yeah," Holly added. "I understand that this isn't exactly the most exciting place to be, but we figure out ways to have fun," she said as she turned to look at Wade.

Jada nodded. "I'll think about it. Sometimes I do get seriously bored. It's like, oh my gawd, could this place get any lamer?" She rolled her eyes again and almost seemed to pout.

"So you saw someone go into the rec room late last night," Missy said, getting them back on track. "Do you have any idea what time that might have been? Something to give us an idea about what time this happened."

Jada shrugged. "I'm not sure. Maybe 11:00 or so?"

Holly nodded. "Okay, so now we know when they were here." It wasn't much, but it was a start. Granted, Jada could be lying, but the way she explained what happened made Holly believe her. It was as if she'd gotten a glimpse behind that tough girl facade and seen the insecure girl who was hiding behind it.

Holly knew the type because she'd seen other kids at school that were the same way. Their world was being turned upside down and that caused them to do the only thing they knew to do, act as if none of it bothered them, when in reality, it was the exact opposite. Inside, they were like scared little kids.

"What did you do after you saw the person walk into the rec room?" Missy asked, one brow raised.

"I came back inside the house. Like I said, I thought it was Holly going in to decorate, even though she didn't turn on the lights. I went to the kitchen to get something to drink and I saw Jordan. He said he was getting you some water because you had a headache."

Missy nodded. "I remember that. Oh, honey. I'm sorry." She reached out and touched Jada's arm.

"It's okay, not your fault," Jada mumbled. Her hard exterior seemed to be cracking even more.

"Who would want to stop this party?" Holly asked. "I'm having a hard time understanding why someone would want to do this." She shook her head and her mind flashed to the sour look Jodi had given them when they'd mentioned Fiona's party.

"I might be able to give you another person to check into," Missy said. "I'd hate to think she was capable of doing something like this, but I've learned in the past few years you just never know what someone may do."

"Who's that?" Wade asked.

"Her name is Michelle Owens. She usually holds their annual family reunion here around this time of year, but it's never exactly the same time. She showed up after I gave you the room and said she wanted it this weekend. I understand she just assumed it would be available, since it's never been an issue before, but this year..." Missy let her sentence trail off.

"This year I had the room," Holly finished.

"Exactly," Missy nodded. "It's probably worth looking into."

Holly nodded and turned to Wade. "Looks like we know what the next step is. Are you driving, or am I?"

CHAPTER FOURTEEN

As Holly and Wade climbed into Wade's car, he shook his head. "I don't know about this one, Holly. It seems a bit of a stretch that someone would do this just because you got the room first." He buckled his seat belt and then turned the key in the ignition.

"I know," Holly admitted. "But think about how often people do far worse things over something really trivial. It's still a possibility, and we need to check out everyone we can think of."

Her mind flashed back to Jodi and she wondered where she might have been last night. There was no real reason to think she had anything to do with it other than the fact she'd acted so odd when Brigid and Holly had met her at the grocery store.

Brigid may have thought her behavior was normal, but she probably didn't have an outsider's perspective. Holly had seen the mixture of emotions that had played across the woman's face. They looked like anger, jealousy, and rage to her, which were not exactly normal friendly emotions.

"You have a point," he said. "I just wish they would have left your party alone. You worked so hard, and did so much, it's not fair for it to have been destroyed like that. This seems like it's punishing you more than Fiona, since she doesn't even know it's happening. Whoever did this was the lowest of the low, no doubt about that."

He turned onto Pecan Street and then slowed down. "Missy said it should be along in here," he said as he started searching for house numbers. "Hopefully this place will be easy to find."

"Right there," Holly said, pointing. She spotted the big black numbers on the house beside the door, "623 Pecan." There was no mistaking it. "Now we just have to hope she's home."

"Well, there's a car in the driveway, so I'm willing to bet someone is," he said as he pulled up and parked. The curtains were open and a dog was running around in the backyard. "Let's go see." He unbuckled his seat belt and started getting out.

"I can't believe I'm out here worrying about this when I should be fixing the party," Holly sighed. "I know Brigid said she'd take care of it, but I didn't want her to have to. That was the whole point. I wanted to do this all on my own, to prove to myself that I could. I don't feel like that anymore."

"You know she doesn't mind," Wade said as they walked up to the house. "And it's certainly not your fault any of this happened. The blame lies solely on whoever did this. It doesn't say anything bad about you. The party was set up and ready. You did that."

"I know," Holly responded. "But Brigid had plans today. Now she's had to put them off to fix this." It really angered Holly, and the more she had time to think about it, the madder she got. It felt like a bubble rising up in her chest, coaxing her to scream and yell, to voice her frustrations at the world.

"Well, in that case we better figure out who did it," Wade said as they stopped in front of the door. He may have been right, but that didn't quell the anger deep within Holly's chest. She felt like she might burst from it at any moment.

She lifted her hand and pushed on the doorbell button. They heard it ring inside and the sound of someone shuffling towards the door. In a moment, a woman who appeared to be in her mid-50's answered the door.

"May I help you?" she asked. Her brown hair was half curled, as if she'd been interrupted in the middle of doing it.

"I'm sorry to bother you, but are you Michelle Owens?" Holly asked. She reminded herself that she needed to stay calm. There was no point in getting angry at someone who hadn't been a party to what happened.

"I am," Michelle said suspiciously. "And who are you?"

"I'm Wade, and this is Holly," Wade interjected. "We were told that you were upset you didn't get to use the rec room at the church. Is that true?"

The way the woman eyed them agitated Holly. She didn't know why, but she felt the urge to jerk the screen door open and shake Michelle until she told them what they wanted to know. She balled her hands into fists to keep from reaching for the door handle.

"Of course," Michelle scoffed. "I've held our family reunion there for the past seven years. Now I've had to move it. I think that gives me plenty of reason to be upset."

"Were you so upset that you'd break into the rec room to destroy the other person's party?" Holly found herself snapping. She knew she was pushing it with the tone of her voice, but she couldn't help it. If this woman was so angry with her because she'd booked the room first and decided to ruin everything, she was going to get some attitude from Holly. There was no holding in the fire that was burning deep within her belly. It was stoked by the woman's irritation and now it was starting to burn hot.

"What are you talking about?" the woman asked, pausing. All the color seemed to drain from her face. She pushed the screen door open and stepped out onto the porch with them. "Someone destroyed their party?" Her voice was soft, all traces of suspicion and annoyance gone. It was like a wet blanket had been draped on the fire within Holly once she saw the concern expressed on the woman's face.

97

"Yes, ma'am," Wade continued, glancing at Holly. "Someone had a key, was able to get in, and completely destroyed everything. Friends of Holly's are working hard to fix it before it's time for the party. We decided to try and figure out who did it."

By the way he kept glancing over at Holly, he obviously thought she'd been acting out of character, and she had been. But now she was beginning to see she'd been wrong.

"It wasn't me," Michelle said as she shook her head vehemently. "I was here with my husband from 5:00 on last night. We didn't go anywhere or do anything." She paused, looking at Holly a little closer now. She seemed to understand her small outburst, and she gave her a sympathetic look. "Is there anything I can do to help?"

Holly shook her head. "No, but thank you. I'm sorry I reserved the room for the same day you wanted it," she sighed. "But I didn't know and with the weather possibly turning soon…"

"I understand," Michelle said, her voice much kinder now. "That was the exact reason I planned it for this weekend. Don't worry, I found somewhere else that will do just fine. I sent out a message to everyone that I had to change the plans slightly this year. No big deal. Wait, aren't you the girl from the bookstore?" she asked.

Holly had thought the woman looked familiar, but hadn't been sure. "Yes, I am," she nodded. "I'm throwing a party for Fiona, the one who owns the store."

"I've always loved that little shop," she said. "I hope she expands someday in the future. I just love going in there and browsing." She looked at them both again before continuing. "Well, I hope you find out who ruined your party. I understand just how much goes into planning one. People don't realize the sheer amount of time and money that can go into hosting something like that. Good for you for doing that for her."

"Thank you," Holly said. "You have a good day." Holly and Wade turned and headed back to the car in silence. Holly wasn't sure what

Wade was thinking, but she knew her mind was working overtime.

She didn't want to automatically assume that Jodi had a hand in the destruction of Fiona's party, but who else could it be? It wasn't as if there were that many people who even knew about it, let alone could gain access to Missy's keys. But as she opened the car door and climbed inside, she was struck with the idea that perhaps that was the problem.

Was she limiting her focus because she assumed not many people knew about the party? Of course, those who had signed the sheet saying they wanted to attend would know, but what if they'd told others? After all, it was a small town. Maybe there had been more talk about it than she realized. But if that were the case, that meant they had many more possible suspects than she'd originally thought.

"Well, now what?" Wade asked as he started the car. "We're out of suspects."

"Not exactly," Holly admitted. "I have one more idea, but we're going to have to talk to Deputy Keegan. I don't know where this woman lives." She began to explain her interaction with Jodi at Willard's and how she didn't think the woman was as good a friend as Brigid claimed.

"Seems like a reasonable next step," he said as he turned the corner. "So do we head to the sheriff's department?"

"I think so. Even if she's out on patrol, dispatch can radio to her and find out where she is," she nodded. "But first, can we grab something to eat? I never had time to eat, and I'm hungry." She looked at the time and saw it was getting close to lunch.

"Absolutely," he nodded. "Why don't we go to the Chinese buffet? My treat."

"Perfect," Holly said happily. "I could really go for an egg roll right now."

"Me, too," he said. "But I think I'd like to have a whole stack of them." He gave her a playful grin as they headed towards the restaurant.

CHAPTER FIFTEEN

Wade pulled into the parking lot at the local Chinese restaurant and began to look for a parking space. "It amazes me how busy this place always seems to be," Wade mused. "It's way past lunch time, but I guess everyone loves good Chinese food."

"You have to admit that it's one of the best places to eat in Cottonwood Springs," Holly said as Wade finally found a spot to park. "Not that the other places aren't good, but it's nice to have a change of pace once in a while." Holly loved a good burger as much as anyone, but she couldn't resist an order of spicy Emperor Chicken.

"It is," he nodded as he put the car in park. "And I love the buffet. Anytime I can eat all I want, I'm a happy guy," he said with a grin.

"Something has to fill that bottomless pit you call a stomach," she teased as they climbed out of the car. Holly was trying to force herself to relax, but she could feel her shoulders bunching up with worry. She knew Brigid had said she'd take care of the party arrangements, but what if there just wasn't enough time?

If she was going to have to cancel the party, she didn't want to do it at the last minute. That would be rude. She was torn between wanting to cancel the party and continuing with the investigation.

"Look, I know you're worried about the party," Wade said as they walked towards the restaurant. "But it will be okay. You know that, right?"

"No, I don't," Holly admitted. He opened the door for her and they stepped inside. There were a couple of men who appeared to be taking a late lunch waiting to be seated before them. "I'm really thinking of calling it off."

"Don't do that," Wade insisted. The men followed a server to a table, leaving them next in line to be seated. "It's going to work out."

"Just the two of you?" the woman asked as she approached.

"Yes, ma'am," Wade said with a nod. The woman turned to look around the dining area before looking back at them. "Is a booth okay?"

Wade and Holly nodded and the woman instructed them to follow her. She laid two menus on the table and then waited for them to take a seat. She took their drink order and promised to be back soon.

"I wish I had as much faith as you do," Holly said when they were finally alone. "But I don't. I put so much into this party and for someone to do what they did…" she let her sentence trail off because her throat began to tighten. She wasn't sure if her impending tears were from anger or sadness. Maybe both.

"Whoever did this didn't ruin everything," Wade pointed out. "When I went in with Levi, he noticed that most of the decorations themselves were still okay. They're going to have a lot of help too. Don't worry about that part, let's just focus on finding the culprit."

Holly nodded. She knew he wouldn't lie to her. He truly believed it would be okay. She decided then and there that she wouldn't let her emotions get the best of her. She'd put her entire focus into finding out who had done it and not on feeling sorry for herself. Anyway, that wouldn't help the situation at all.

She'd let her anger get the best of her when they'd walked up to Michelle Owen's house, and she'd been wrong. Just the thought that she almost yelled at a woman who was completely innocent made her stomach want to turn. That wasn't who she was. She was a better person that that.

"I think I'm going to stick with the buffet," Wade finally said. "I like it all so much, it's hard to choose just one thing."

Holly looked over the menu, doing her best to stay focused on what she was doing now. After a quick look at it she said, "I think I will too."

Almost as soon as they'd set the menus down, the waitress returned with their drinks. She took their order, and soon they were at the buffet filling their plates. While she was helping herself to the food items on display, Holly tried to focus on the case. They'd already crossed two people off their list. She still wanted to look into Jodi, the woman from the grocery store. Considering she hadn't seemed happy about Fiona's success, it was a logical next step.

She sat down in the booth and realized that Wade was already there, shoveling beef lo mein into his mouth. He looked up at her and grinned. "Sorry, I was hungry."

She chuckled. "It's fine. I know better than to stand in the way of you and your food."

"Tell me again what the plan is after we finish eating," he said as he continued to dig in. "I want to make sure I understand."

"We're going to go see Deputy Keegan at the sheriff's station and ask her where Jodi Young lives. Then we'll go visit her and see what she has to say for herself." Holly unwrapped her silverware from the napkin and began to eat.

"You sound pretty sure it's her," he observed.

"Who else could it be? And it makes sense. This woman and

Fiona have been friends on and off all these years. She said that she and Fiona had a fight before she moved away. Maybe she decided this was her opportunity to get back at Fiona for whatever they fought about. It's not really a big stretch," she said with a shrug.

"Promise me you'll keep calm?" Wade asked carefully. She knew he wasn't accusing her of anything, but she could tell he was worried about her, and that meant a lot.

"I promise," she said. "I'm sorry. I know I was being a jerk for a second back there."

"It's okay, you're usually so nice that I think you can get away with it this time," he said with a wink. "I was just worried about you."

"I'm sorry," she said. "I know I acted out of character. I'm good though. I swear. You don't have to worry about me."

He studied her for a moment, searching her eyes. Finally, he must have seen what he was looking for. "Okay, I believe you."

They continued to eat and chat about other things, allowing Holly to take her mind off of the party for a little while. It was nice and at the same time she was able to reframe her thoughts.

She'd gotten a little angry back there for a while, and she didn't want to act like that anymore. Having a moment to breathe helped her step back and see exactly what Wade had been concerned about. Her chest filled with a warm love for him, knowing he had been there for her like that.

Her cell phone rang and she pulled it out and saw that it was Fiona. With a nervous stutter, she answered.

"I'm so sorry if I woke you up," Fiona said quickly into the phone. "But I just had to tell you."

"Oh, okay," Holly said as she stumbled over her words. She'd almost forgotten she told Fiona she was going home to take a nap.

"What is it?"

"I just got a call from the Green Butterfly Clothing people. They said my designs are ready to be seen and released. They want to fly me there to see them!" She squealed the last few words because she couldn't contain herself anymore.

"Are you serious?" Holly gasped.

"Yes," Fiona was breathless on the other end. "I want to ask Brigid if she'll go with me. Do you think she can? I thought I'd leave you in charge of the bookstore, and if Linc can hold down the B & B for a little while…"

"Are you kidding? I'm sure she'd love to go," Holly said. She could barely contain her excitement about being in charge of the bookstore.

"Okay, I'll call her and ask. Thank you, Holly, for everything." Her words were so sincere that it brought a tear to Holly's eyes.

"Any time," was all she managed to choke out.

When she finished the call, she looked up to see Wade smiling at her. "I heard. You get to run the bookstore while she and Brigid go to California?"

"I guess so," Holly said, stunned. "I can't believe it."

"Why? You know that place better than anyone," he observed. "She'd be crazy to pick someone else."

"Still, I'm going to be the boss for a little while. That just feels so strange," Holly admitted. "Oh, while I'm thinking of it, I should probably call the sheriff's department and make sure Deputy Keegan is there before we drive over."

"That's probably a smart idea," he said with a nod. "You do that while I keep enjoying this lo mein."

Holly searched for the phone number for the sheriff's department on her cell phone contact list and then hit call. After a short conversation, she was told that Deputy Keegan was, in fact, at the station.

"Great. Would you please tell her that Holly and Wade will be coming to see her in about twenty or thirty minutes? Thanks." She put her phone away and lifted her fork. "Now that's taken care of."

"And now it's time for you to eat," he said insistently. "Can't have you running around and not eating."

Holly shook her head. "Not all of us have metabolisms like hummingbirds," she said with a raised brow.

"Keep trying, you'll get there," he said with a grin.

"I think my stomach would explode if I ate as much as you do," she muttered.

"Nah, it wouldn't. You might feel like it would, but you'd be okay," he reassured her.

CHAPTER SIXTEEN

"That was good," Wade said as they pulled out of the parking lot. "Now I think I can concentrate on our investigation again." He gave her a teasing look as they drove across town. He was forever making jokes about being hungry, and he knew it drove Holly nuts.

"I'm so glad you could get your belly full so we could focus," she teased back. She had to admit, she felt much better now that she'd eaten. Her spirit seemed lighter, as if she'd been wearing a weighted vest and had taken it off. Maybe it was the food, maybe it was Fiona's good news. Whatever it was, she was grateful for it.

"Let's just get to the sheriff's department before your belly empties and we need to make another stop for you to refuel."

"Hey, I'm a growing boy," he said with a mischievous grin.

"Keep it up and you'll start growing out," she laughed. "Then you'd have a tough time fitting into your baseball uniform."

"I'll go on a run tonight," he said, dismissing her concerns. "It'll be fine."

After a short drive, they pulled into the sheriff station's parking lot. There weren't many cars parked there, which told Holly that there weren't many officers inside the building. They climbed out of the car while Holly was lost in her thoughts. She needed to find out who did this to her party. How could she relax until she had?

"I still think it's kind of cool that Brigid's a consultant for them," Wade said as they walked towards the station. Holly looked up at the older building and thought about it. The fact that Brigid wasn't a cop, but had managed to make herself indispensable to the sheriff's office was kind of cool.

"I guess it kind of is," Holly said. "Honestly, she's been doing stuff like that for as long as I've known her. Can you imagine a Brigid that wasn't investigating something?" She laughed at the thought.

"I thought she was going to get her notebook and start taking down suspects when she couldn't find her favorite kitchen spatula the other day." Holly could still picture it, and it made her smile. Brigid hadn't let up that day either until she'd narrowed down where the spatula had last been seen and then figured out that it had fallen down between two kitchen counters.

"Brigid has a favorite spatula?" Wade chuckled as he opened the door for Holly. "Adults can be so weird sometimes. My mom has a favorite pan that she almost always cooks with, so I guess I understand about Brigid and her spatula."

Stepping inside, they were met with fall decorations. "Wow, it looks great in here," Holly said as she looked around. There was a leaf garland along the counter and lights wrapped with it and a small hay bale in the corner with a scarecrow sitting on it.

Holly thought he must have not been a very good scarecrow, because a crow was on the hay bale beside him. There were other splashes of fall leaves around the room, tucked around lights, and wherever else there was a little room.

"You like it?" Deputy Keegan asked as she walked towards them. "I got a little tired of seeing the same stuff every day. Thought the place could use a little sprucing up. Nobody seemed to mind when I suggested it, so I just took it upon myself to do it."

"It looks really good," Holly nodded, impressed. "You aren't busy, are you?"

"Nope, and the sheriff told me you might be needing my help. He said you guys had some sort of a situation going on and were doing a bit of poking around. I guess Brigid is calling in one of her many favors," she shrugged.

"Not that I think she really needs to. I know I can speak for the sheriff when I say that if you guys need anything, we're always here to do what we can. No questions asked. What can I help you with?'

Holly thought it was great to have friends like Deputy Keegan and Sheriff Davis. He'd been the one who had actually made it possible for her to stay with Brigid in the first place. They may not be related, but he was like family to her.

"I need the address of a woman by the name of Jodi Young. I think she may have been the one to destroy the party." Holly was glad she could finally say it without wanting to strangle someone. It meant to her she was making some progress in controlling her emotions.

"Whoa, whoa, wait a minute. Destroyed the party? I didn't hear about that part," Deputy Keegan said, her eyes going wide. "What happened? Tell me everything. Do I need to file a report?"

"It might come to that," Holly said. "But right now, I need to figure out who did it. I want to know where this woman was last night. And if it wasn't her, I'll have to find another possible suspect."

She hoped it didn't come to that because she had absolutely no clue at this point who else might be a suspect. Maybe someone had done it because they were mad at her, but she had no idea who that could be, and she was running out of suspects.

"Do you want me to come with you?" Deputy Keegan asked. "This seems a little on the serious side."

"Honestly, we've done this quite a bit," Wade confessed with a wince. "I promise, it's not as intimidating as it sounds. We've gotten pretty good at shaping our questions so it doesn't even seem like we're questioning them. Besides, most people are under the impression we wouldn't be able to do anything about it, even if they do tell us."

It was sad, but unfortunately true. Holly couldn't count how many times people had underestimated them.

Deputy Keegan looked at them both for a long moment, as if she wasn't sure if she should believe them. Holly could see she was debating whether to let this go or be official about it. After all, she could always step in and take over the investigation if she felt it was necessary. Finally, she shook her head. "Don't get in any trouble," she sighed.

"We'll be fine," Holly said, waving off her concerns. She felt like after she'd dealt with the Oracle, she could handle this and practically anything else.

Deputy Keegan froze. "Wait a minute, I just remembered something." She squinted as she apparently tried to recall what it was. "I heard something somewhere. Where was I?"

"What do you mean?" Holly asked, confused.

"I heard someone talk about a party..." she began. "Oh, I remember, I was at that clothing store. The fancy one. Anyway, I don't think the owner realized how loud she was being, but I heard her conversation. She said something about wrecking a party. I wasn't paying any attention at first, so I'm not sure if it was yours, but how many parties could possibly be going on?"

Wade and Holly exchanged a look. "You'd be surprised," she said.

"I saw Fiona in the dress shop. She'd bought something and was just leaving. We said hello to each other, but that was about it. You know how it is when you see someone in passing. But after she left the shop the owner seemed to act strangely. I don't know how else to describe it. She and a friend went into the back room and started speaking in hushed tones about a party and wishing it would get ruined or something like that," she said, shrugging.

"Still, if you're trying to get to the bottom of this, check her out and let me know. I'm not sure Sheriff Davis understood the seriousness of what happened. It sounds to me like whoever did this committed some serious violations of the law. I wish I'd seen the damage myself."

"If there are laws that were broken, then I guess you're right," Wade shrugged. "We didn't break the law, they did."

"Brigid and some other people have been cleaning it up," Holly said. "So it won't look like it did."

"Jordan was taking pictures," Wade said. "And he was doing a good job of it, too. He'd have what you need."

"I'll go over to the church after we're done here. I'll get that address for you, and I'll also write down the info on that store owner." She tapped the desk with her hand before turning and heading to a nearby computer. "You guys can come in and sit down," she said as she motioned to the chairs in front of the desk.

They rounded the counter that divided the waiting area from the desks for the deputies.

"I didn't realize you shopped at Chic Boutique," Holly said as she sat down.

"Honestly, I don't. That was the second time I'd ever been in there, but I had a special occasion and needed something nice to wear, so I thought I'd give it a shot." Deputy Keegan said as she flushed a little.

"Oh, really?" Holly asked, raising her brow. "It's like that now, huh?" she giggled.

Deputy Keegan shrugged before turning a deeper shade of red. "Maybe."

Wade shook his head. "Girls," he muttered. The slight smirk on his face said he didn't really mind.

"Okay, here's the first one," she said as she wrote down an address. "This is for Jodi." She wrote the name quickly and then circled it. "And this is the shop owner. Her name is Jenny Crabtree."

"I've heard of her," Wade said as he rolled his eyes. "And nothing I've heard was good."

"We'll go see her after we see Jodi," Holly said.

"And you'll let me know if you find anything out? If there's enough damage, and we know they had a key without permission, we can charge them." Deputy Keegan had been ready to hand over the paper, but withheld it as she waited for Holly's answer.

"I'll call you as soon as I find out something," Holly swore. "I won't do anything after that but try to keep an eye on whoever it is."

"That's good enough for me," Deputy Keegan said as she handed the paper over. "Good luck. I hope I hear from you." She gave them a big grin that seemed to say she was confident she would.

"I hope so too," Holly said as she took the slip of paper.

CHAPTER SEVENTEEN

"Are you sure you want to visit this Jodi woman first?" Wade asked as they walked back to his car. "It sounds like this other woman may have actually threatened the party. If she was talking about ruining a party and then yours gets ruined..." he let his sentence trail off to make a point.

"I know, and you're not wrong," Holly agreed. "But in reality, she could have been talking about anything, right? Deputy Keegan didn't specifically hear her say Fiona's party. How do we even know she knew about Fiona's party?"

Holly knew she was stretching it, but that didn't make it untrue. There was a family reunion happening the day of Fiona's party, so why couldn't there have been another party? As far as they knew she could have been talking about a party in another town.

"I guess you're right," Wade admitted. "And you know this woman has a thing against Fiona. She probably is the better one to visit next. But we'll go over to Chic Boutique once we're done and see if this Jenny woman is there before we go by her house. I'm pretty sure she doesn't have too many people working for her. I think I heard that she likes to do it all herself."

"Good idea," Holly said, nodding. "We're starting to run out of time. I don't think I'll be able to relax if we don't figure out who did this. I'd be too worried they'd come busting down the door, equipped with some new way to ruin the party."

She could just see it now. Some strange person whipping the door open and rushing inside with a fire extinguisher, spraying everything. If someone decided to do something like that, it would definitely put a damper on things, even if it did make it obvious who was to blame for it.

"I'd hope they weren't that type of person, but I see your point. Whoever did this was a very determined individual. If they really wanted to ruin the party completely, they may still have a backup plan. Heck, they may have a backup plan to their backup plan," Wade said as he continued to drive.

"You have no idea. Remember me calling you the other day after dinner and telling you about someone canceling my orders?" she asked. Remembering that day, she wished she could go back in time and warn herself. Then she could have done all the decorating today and Brigid could have gone shopping and to visit Melanie like she'd intended to do.

"That's right!" he said. "I'd forgotten all about that. It has to be the same person. It's too bad the bakery and deli didn't have the number of whoever called, and we could run a reverse search on it."

"That's actually a really good idea. Maybe we should look into that after we check out these two women. And you know what? I almost wonder if whoever did it planned to do this the whole time?" she mused aloud.

"Like they planned to cancel the food without me knowing and then came to the room to destroy the decorations." The idea put a chill through her. The idea that anyone could be that mean was beyond her. Who would want to destroy a party? Didn't everyone love a good party? Holly couldn't imagine anyone that didn't.

"This should be it," Wade said as they pulled up in front of a single story, ranch style home. The yard was covered in a blanket of leaves, and the chain link fence around the back yard had leaves piled up in the corners where the wind had blown and deposited them.

"What's this lady like?" he asked as he parked and turned off the engine.

"I got the feeling she had another side to her," Holly said. "I think she wants to appear like she's got everything together, but inside she's falling apart." It wasn't a judgment, but more of an observation. If anything, Holly felt a little sorry for her.

When they got to the door and Holly raised her hand to knock on it, it opened. "Do I know you?" Jodi asked as she peered out the screen door. "You were with Brigid the other day at the store. It's Holly, right?"

"Yes, ma'am," Holly said. "And this is Wade. If you're not too busy, I'd like to ask you a couple of questions."

"Sure, but let's do it out here," Jodi said as she stepped outside. "I've been cooped up in the house all morning, and it feels good to be outside." She walked over to the stairs that led to the porch and sat down. Wade looked at Holly and shrugged before doing the same.

"I don't know how much help I could be, but what did you want to ask?" Jodi asked after they both took a seat.

A couple of sparrows chased a blue jay out of a tree while Holly considered her words. "You said you and Fiona weren't on speaking terms. May I ask why?" She knew it was a fairly direct question, but it needed to be asked.

"Actually, I've been thinking about that a lot the past couple of days," she said. "And I've come to the conclusion it was a stupid reason. Most of it was jealousy on my part, I'm afraid."

"I don't quite understand," Holly admitted.

"It's no secret Fiona's talented. She always has been. I guess I always knew she'd do something amazing, and I wouldn't. I always felt like I was in her shadow," Jodi shrugged.

"You said you've been thinking about it," Wade interjected. "What made you start thinking about it?"

Jodi paused and seemed to choose her words carefully. "When I saw Holly and Brigid at the store, I wasn't exactly happy with the news that Fiona was hitting it big. Then to hear there was a party being thrown in her honor?" she scoffed. "My head was ready to explode."

"You sound like you feel differently now," Wade observed. Holly thought he was right. She didn't seem quite the same as she had the other day.

"I do," Jodi admitted. "I'm still working on it, but I think I've had an epiphany. I've had a rough time for quite a while, but when I look back on it, it's my own fault."

"What do you mean?" Holly asked. She wasn't exactly sure what Jodi meant by that. But then again, she didn't really know the woman.

"I always thought I deserved something. Looking back, that's how it started. I felt I was entitled to something, even though I didn't know what. But all I did by acting as though others owed me was push them away. I wasn't being very giving, but I certainly had no trouble taking from them."

Jodi reached down and picked up a maple leaf. She twirled it in her fingers before continuing. "My family has been torn apart, because I thought I deserved things without having to work for them. My friendships disintegrated because I thought all their attention should be on me. That's where I was wrong. Why should anyone pay attention to me if I'm not willing to pay attention to them?"

"That's heavy stuff," Holly said. "So you're saying you weren't at the church last night?"

Jodi turned her head slightly and frowned. "No, I was on a video chat with my son last night and then I went to bed. Why do you ask?"

"Last night someone destroyed the decorations for Fiona's surprise party," Wade said. "And they also tried to cancel the cake and food."

Jodi gasped. "You've got to be kidding!"

"I wish I was," Holly admitted. "All the money I spent on it is down the drain. Brigid's trying to fix what she can while we try to find out who may have done this."

"I don't blame you for coming to pay me a visit," Jodi said. "But I promise you it wasn't me. I can't say I didn't want something to happen to her party that day that I saw you. But realizing just how bitter I felt about it made me do some soul-searching." She tapped her finger to her chin. "Wait here a minute," she said as she stood. "I'll be right back."

When she'd disappeared into the house, Wade turned to Holly. "Is this where she gets a gun and shoots us?" he joked.

"Oh, stop," Holly said as she slapped at him. "That's not funny."

"Here," she said as she returned. "I know it's not much but maybe it can help." She thrust two twenty-dollar bills in Holly's hand.

"You don't have to do this. I'll manage," Holly said quickly.

"No, I insist," Jodi said as she held her hand up. "All I ask is that you put in a good word for me with Fiona. Let her know I'm sorry this happened."

"She doesn't know about the party. It was supposed to be a surprise," Holly said as she tucked the money in her pocket. "Hey, why don't you come?"

Jodi seemed shocked. "You want me to come to the party?" she asked.

"Why not? If she doesn't know you're in town yet, you just might be a surprise. I bet she'd be happy to see you," Wade offered.

"I wouldn't want to impose," Jodi said looking down.

"Nonsense," Holly said as she stood up. "I insist." She explained what she had planned for the party, Fiona's surprise entrance, and what time that should be. "You need to be there at least ten minutes before that, so she doesn't suspect anything."

"Not a problem," Jodi said with a grin. "Thank you."

"Just patch things up with Fiona and learn from your mistakes," Holly said. "I bet you'll be surprised how your luck may turn around."

CHAPTER EIGHTEEN

"Next stop, Chic Boutique," Holly said as they climbed back in Wade's car. "Hopefully she's there. That would make it so much easier."

"True, but how are we going to approach her on this? It's not like we heard her saying those things. It's all just hearsay." Wade looked a little frustrated by the thought.

"We'll figure it out. We always do," she reminded him just as her phone rang. "It's Brigid," she said before answering.

"Holly, two things," Brigid began after she answered. "I'll start with the important thing first. Missy has a clue that may help."

"I'm all ears," Holly said. "At this point, anything that can help us out would be wonderful."

"Missy went through her office and found that out of the four keys she has for the rec room, number three is missing. She said it's on a Colorado keychain and has a piece of grey tape on it with the number three written on it."

"Okay, so what you're saying is if we find the key, that means we found the person who got in last night," Holly pieced together.

"That's the idea," Brigid agreed. "Obviously, don't be reckless. Don't go searching through people's stuff or anything looking for it."

"Of course not," Holly said. "But it's still something to watch out for. What else did you want to tell me?"

"I just thought I would ask how you felt about me going to California with Fiona? She said she asked you, but I wanted to hear it from you." Brigid sounded apprehensive.

"I think you should go. I'm sure Linc and I can handle the B & B," she said. "You should go with your sister and enjoy sunny California. I mean, you used to live there, so you know how sunny it is."

"I do, and in that case, I'll go," Brigid said, sounding relieved. "And don't worry about the party, it's coming together. It will be ready in time. Actually, I think you're going to be shocked when you get here."

"Really? Why?" Holly asked.

"You just finish up and you'll see later," Brigid said cryptically. "If you find whoever did this…"

"Don't worry, we already have a plan. Deputy Keegan is on standby as we speak. If we figure it out, we're to call her immediately." Holly knew Brigid needed to know the plan so she wouldn't think Holly was going to do something reckless.

"Good, that's what I like to hear. Good luck, and I'll see you in a little while."

Holly punched end and put her phone in her purse. She repeated the description of the key to Wade, who nodded.

"We'll keep an eye out for it, but I highly doubt whoever did this would leave it lying around," he said.

"You never know," Holly shrugged. "Sometimes people do stupid things. We're banking on the fact that they don't suspect we're looking for them."

"That's true," Wade agreed. He started the car and pulled away from Jodi's house. "They might think you're too busy trying to fix the party or something."

"If they even know who I am," Holly pointed out. "I don't know if I've ever seen the woman who owns Chic Boutique." Holly had gone in there once with Brigid but felt awkward and out of place. She'd never gone back.

"I don't know, but we'll find out," he said. "Mom goes in there once in a while, but she said the woman behind the counter usually ignores her."

"Sounds like she got lucky," Holly chuckled.

Before long they were pulling up in front of the store. "Here we are," Wade said. "I also have a plan, just follow my lead." Before she could say anything, Wade climbed out of the car.

"Wade, wait," she said hurrying to follow. "What are you doing?"

"I have an idea," he repeated, his hand on the door. "Just trust me, okay?" His eyes were wide and pleading, tugging at her heartstrings.

"Okay, fine," Holly said.

Wade smiled and opened the door for her. "After you," he said.

"Now isn't that sweet," the woman behind the counter said as she walked around in front of it. "You don't see that every day."

"Thank you," he said with his handsome grin. Holly could tell he was laying it on thick. "I thought I'd bring my beautiful girlfriend in to buy a new dress. She has a party to go to today."

"Isn't that wonderful," she said clapping her hands together. "Well, I'm the owner here. My name is Jenny. Is there anything special we're looking for? A color or style?" She moved to the dress rack and started sliding the hangers. "I bet I could guess your size too."

Meanwhile, Holly was staring at Wade, her mouth hanging open. He'd completely thrown her off guard by saying he was buying her a dress. He knew she wasn't a fan of them. She had a feeling this was all a part of his plan.

"She's more into darker colors," Wade said as he began looking at the dresses himself. "What about that dark blue one?"

"Oh, good choice," Jenny said. "This is probably about her size." She pulled a dress from the rack and held it up in front of Holly. "What do you think, honey?"

"I- It's very pretty," she stammered. "But I don't know if it would look very good on me."

"Nonsense, you're a beautiful girl. At least try it on and let's see," Jenny said as she held it out.

"Yes, please try it on," Wade said with an innocent smile. Holly could see by the twinkle in his eyes he was getting a kick out of this.

"Um, okay," Holly said as the woman handed her the dress.

"Right back there," Jenny said, point towards the dressing rooms. "We'll be waiting for you."

Holly cast Wade a glance promising to get even with him and then made her way to the dressing room. She had to admit that the dress was beautiful. There was no harm in at least seeing what it looked like on her.

After slipping it on, she zipped it up as far as she could. It fit her perfectly. No matter what, Jenny was good at sizing people up.

Taking a deep breath, Holly stepped out of the dressing room.

"Oh, you look beautiful," Jenny gasped as they turned back to Holly. "Your hair looks so much brighter."

"She's right," Wade said softly. "You're gorgeous. I- I mean, not that you aren't normally. It's just..."

"She knows what you mean," Jenny said as Wade fumbled over his words. Holly could feel a blush rising in her cheeks with the way Wade was staring at her. "Now, let's see here." Jenny went behind her and zipped the dress the rest of the way up. She adjusted the material so that it laid flat against her.

"Perfect. I think with that neckline you need some sort of a simple necklace. You could wear your hair down and it would look nice. Are you going to that family reunion that's planned?" Jenny asked.

"Uh, no," Wade said as he came back to himself. "We're going to the surprise party for Fiona Garcia."

Jenny seemed to freeze, rooted to the spot. She turned and looked at Wade. "I thought that had been canceled?"

Wade looked at Holly and then back at Jenny. "We haven't heard anything like that. Where on earth would you hear something like that?"

Jenny seemed to catch herself. "Oh, I must have heard it somewhere. Would you two excuse me for one second? You can keep looking around. Just let me know when you're ready." She rushed to the back room and shut the curtain behind her.

Wade hurried over to Holly. "Did you notice that?" he whispered.

"I did. Seems awfully suspicious."

"Go ahead and change. I'm still going to buy that dress for you," he said with a wink. "But I think we may be on to something."

Holly nodded and hurried back to the dressing room. Once she'd changed clothes, she stepped back outside. She saw Wade standing by the cash register. He waved her over, while holding a finger up to his lips. When she joined him, he pointed to something by the register.

Right there, tucked up to the side of the cash register was a single key on a Colorado keychain. Wade carefully flipped it over to reveal a piece of grey tape with the number three written on it.

"Call Keegan," he mouthed. "I'll take care of paying for this."

Holly nodded and started heading for the door. It was probably best to step outside to make the call, so Jenny wouldn't hear her. Just as she got to the door, Wade called to Jenny. "I think we're ready to pay," he said.

As soon as Holly was outside, she began to dial Deputy Keegan's number. She answered on the second ring.

"Keegan," she said abruptly.

"Jenny Crabtree has the key missing from Missy's office next to the cash register at Chic Boutique," Holly said quickly. "She also seemed to be under the impression that the surprise party had been canceled."

"That's interesting," Deputy Keegan said. "I'm already on my way. Keep an eye on her."

Holly agreed before hanging up and going back inside. Jenny was folding the dress up in tissue paper before placing it in the bag. They were talking politely about the weather as Holly approached. Still holding her phone in her hand, she started recording a video while pretending to scroll through her email.

"Tell me," Holly began, trying to think of the best way to start the conversation. "Who said the party was canceled again?" she asked. "I'm just asking because I want to make sure they know that it's still happening. You know, so they can be sure to join us. It would be a shame for someone to miss it."

Her voice didn't give a hint at the anger she was feeling towards the woman. She realized she was standing in front of the person who had ruined all her hard work.

"Oh, uh, I can't remember," she said waving her hand. "It's not that important."

"Actually, it kind of is," Holly insisted. "I mean, imagine thinking a party you were supposed to go to was canceled, but it really hadn't been. So you didn't go and then your friend thinks you're not being supportive and gets angry at you. I don't think that would be good for anyone."

Jenny narrowed her eyes at Holly. "Yes, I guess that would be a shame."

Holly waited for a moment and then she said, "Why did you do it?" All the anger she'd felt turned into sadness.

For a moment it looked like Jenny was going to argue with them. But when she saw the look on Holly's face and realized what she'd truly done, her face fell. "I'm sorry."

"Excuse me?" Wade said.

The door to the store opened and Deputy Keegan walked in. She didn't appear to be in a hurry, but you could tell she wasn't someone to be messed with. Holly held up one finger to the deputy before turning back to Jenny.

"What did you say?" she asked, a single tear slipping down her cheek.

"I said I'm sorry," Jenny sighed as her shoulders collapsed. "I admit it. I destroyed the party."

"But why?" Wade asked.

"Because I knew that now I'd never get to carry Fiona's clothing in my store. I wanted us to partner up so we could both be famous. Now, what am I supposed to do?" She looked down at the floor before putting her face in her hands. "I really messed up."

"Yes, you did," Deputy Keegan said as she pulled out her handcuffs. "And you have the right to remain silent." She began to read Jenny her Miranda rights and then radioed for another car. In a few moments another deputy arrived and took Jenny Crabtree away.

"You two did a good job," Deputy Keegan said. "And I'm hoping you were recording her while she was talking?"

"Right here," Holly said as she held up her phone. "I got it all on video."

"Then I guess you did what you set out to do," she said. "You caught the bad guy and from what I hear, Brigid's almost ready over at the rec room. Everything's going to work out after all."

"She should have known better than to mess with Holly," Wade said confidently. "She's beauty and brains in one awesome package."

CHAPTER NINETEEN

Holly checked the time on her phone. It was 5:50. Fiona would be showing up soon, so it was time to get everyone ready. She walked over to the microphone and clicked it on.

"Okay, everyone," she said as she held her hands up and waved them. As the room full of people turned towards her, she lowered her hands and brushed them down the front of her dark blue dress. "Fiona should be showing up any time soon, so we have to turn the lights off. If everyone can find a seat or somewhere they're comfortable standing, we're going to make it dark in here."

Linc walked over to the light switch while people got into position. Many of them were grinning from ear to ear, looking as though they were just as excited as Holly was.

Brigid had done an amazing job with the help of Levi, Missy, and Jordan. The man at the deli, when Brigid had called and told him what happened, had dropped what he was doing and made all new sandwiches at no charge, and he even delivered them. Missy had gone to the store and bought all new balloon bouquets and even added more balloons. They'd been able to save most of the table decorations and the streamers had been replaced. It looked almost exactly as it had before.

Once everyone was settled, Linc switched the lights off. Holly turned to Wade and slipped her hand in his.

"Am I the only one who feels like they're shaking from anticipation?" he whispered.

"I thought that shaking was me?" Holly quipped. They squeezed each other's hands as they waited in the dark for Fiona.

"Headlights," someone called out.

"Here we go," Holly squealed as she turned towards Brigid. Brigid stepped forward and smiled, showing she was excited too.

Everyone watched as the headlights maneuvered through the lot to a parking space. When the lights had been turned off, they heard the sound of car doors.

Holly could just imagine what Fiona was feeling now. Brandon, her husband, had driven her to the church under the pretext that Missy was getting some volunteers together for a new project. They knew she'd always try to help Missy and that would account for the extra cars in the lot. Fiona was probably trying to figure out how to shuffle her schedule around as they walked to the door.

The door handle turned and it was as if you could hear a pin drop in the room. Everyone was frozen with anticipation as the door slowly opened. Fiona was the first one inside, and she reached for the light switch. As she flipped it on, the entire room yelled, "Surprise!" Fiona threw her hands up in shock.

"Oh, my goodness!" she cried out as Brandon grinned and little Aiden squealed in delight.

Holly flipped on the microphone. "Come in, Fiona. We've been waiting for you."

Everyone laughed and Holly noticed Fiona brushing her fingers under her eyes. "What's this about?" she laughed.

"Come here," Holly said as she reached out for her. Fiona made her way around the room and to the front of it where Holly was standing. "You have accomplished so much, Mrs. Fiona Garcia, and we thought it was about time we celebrated that."

"Are you serious?" Fiona asked.

"Absolutely," Brigid said as she stepped forward. "You're an inspiration to all of us."

"That's right," a woman in the crowd called out.

The crowd began to chant, "Speech, speech, speech, speech!"

Fiona took the microphone from Holly and smiled. "Okay, okay, settle down," she said, making everyone laugh. "Let me think of something to say." She stood there a moment, looking down at her feet and Brigid handed her a tissue. Fiona chuckled as she took it and mouthed, "Thank you" before she wiped her face and began to speak.

"I know some of you may have gone to school with me, but I think most of you met me through the bookstore," she began, her hands shaking. "So for those who didn't know me, I was a bit of a nerd in school." A low chuckle went through the room.

"No, it's true," Fiona insisted. "But I was proud of that. I was different and unique and loved to do my own thing, no matter what." She paused, collecting her words. "And then I went to a school to study fashion design. You'd think that would be where you'd really be able to be yourself and create, but that wasn't the case for me. My teacher felt things should be done a certain way. I wasn't loving it, and money was tight, so I quit."

She shrugged. "And because of it, my light ended up dimming. I think it was still as colorful as always, but in a much milder tone. And I would say it was so dim you almost couldn't see it. At least that's how it felt to me."

Fiona turned and looked at Holly. "But then this girl came into my life. She made me start to see myself differently again. She fanned the flames of that old spark that used to be in me and brought it back to life."

Holly reached for Fiona's hand, feeling more tears threatening. *I swear I haven't cried this much in one day in my entire life*, she thought as she smiled at her aunt.

"She believed in me in a way I didn't know I needed. Don't get me wrong, I know all of you did too, but this one was relentless." She squeezed Holly's hand. "And because of that, I was able to put myself out there. Her constant belief in me is what pushed me out of my comfort zone. And now look at me!" She lifted her hands in the air.

"So remember that. Sometimes people may need something they don't know to ask for. If you believe in someone, let them know it. Push them to grow and stand tall in who they are, because we don't need a million people who are all the same. We need one of everyone."

She clicked off the microphone and every person there began to clap. Holly grinned, knowing that Fiona was probably feeling awkward about all the attention she was getting, but not caring one bit. She deserved it. She deserved all of it.

EPILOGUE

"Thanks again for the party, Holly," Fiona said. She was sitting at the kitchen table with Brigid and Linc drinking coffee while Aiden played with Jett and Lucky.

"I was glad I could do it," Holly said. She'd just gotten dressed and was looking for a jacket. "I'm off to pick up Wade and Levi. Jada's leaving tomorrow, so we thought we'd go say goodbye."

"I'm glad you guys got to spend some time with her," Brigid said. "Missy told me she's been much more pleasant the past few weeks. She said she hadn't been totally sure the girl could smile until you guys took her under your wing."

"We just gave her something to do," Holly shrugged. "And it turned out that all those times she'd taken off was because she was finding stuff to sketch. She's really a great artist. She drew an awesome picture of the bookstore I think I'm going to frame and hang there."

"That's wonderful," Brigid smiled. "So did her parents figure things out?"

"Yeah, they're staying together. I guess while she was gone, they did a lot of talking and they've vowed to start again. I hope it works for them," Holly said.

"Me, too," Brigid said. "Do we know what's happened with Jenny Crabtree?"

"Last I heard her court date is coming up soon," Fiona said as she sipped her coffee. "I guess she's hoping to get community service instead of doing jail time."

"Surely it wouldn't be very long if she did get sentenced to do time in jail?" Linc asked.

"I don't know," Fiona shrugged. "Is it mean of me to kind of wish she would get some jail time, though? Just so she's forced to wear a prisoner jumpsuit. Even if it was only a few weeks, I think it would serve her right. I'll never shop at Chic Boutique again, no matter what happens to her."

"I think a lot of people feel that way," Holly said as she bent over to pick up Aiden. "I've heard it's not doing very well."

Brigid shrugged. "That's what happens when you let your ego take over. Did she ever say how she got the key from Missy?"

"Missy told me she admitted to going into her office when she was busy," Fiona supplied. "I guess she saw Missy outside and spoke to her for a little bit before saying she needed to use the restroom. Instead of going to the restroom, she went into Missy's office and swiped the key."

"That's terrible," Linc chimed in. "Taking advantage of someone's generosity like that. I hope Missy isn't still beating herself up over it."

"She's doing better about it," Fiona said. "But she did say that it's made her think twice about what she leaves laying around in plain sight. It never occurred to her that someone would have the audacity to walk into her office like that and take a key from her."

"Well who would?" Brigid asked. "This is Cottonwood Springs. You could almost compare this place to Mayberry on the Andy Griffith TV show. We don't have to lock our doors or look over our shoulders when we walk down the street. You'd think your stuff would be safe inside a church office, of all places."

Everyone nodded in agreement.

"What do you guys have going on today?" Holly asked.

"Nothing," Linc said with a shrug.

"Brigid and I were just talking about our trip to California," Fiona said. "After I leave here, I'm going to meet Jodi. We talked about going to lunch or something."

"How's she doing?" Holly asked. She'd been wondering about her ever since she'd questioned her about the party and her involvement in its destruction.

"Great, actually. She said she and her husband have been talking about her moving home," Fiona said. "I'm glad she was able to move here and for us to patch things up. I think she's finally straightened her life out."

"It can take some people a while," Brigid muttered.

"I don't think some ever learn," Linc added.

"Speaking of the party and your suspects," Brigid said to Holly. "I guess Michelle Owens and Missy now have an agreement that the last Saturday in September is when she'll always have her reunions at the rec room."

Holly laughed. "Well, I guess that's good." She set Aiden back down on the floor. "I think I'm going to head out. If you guys need me, call."

"Okay, love you," they all said in unison.

"Love you all, too," Holly said as she walked out the front door with a huge smile of satisfaction on her face.

LEAVE A REVIEW

I'd really appreciate it you could take a few seconds and leave a review of Holly and the Ruined Party

Just go to the link below. Thank you so much, it means a lot to me ~ Dianne

http://getbook.at/HRP

Paperbacks & Ebooks for FREE

Go to www.dianneharman.com/freepaperback.html and get your FREE copies of Dianne's books and favorite recipes immediately by signing up for her newsletter.

Once you've signed up for her newsletter you're eligible to win three paperbacks. One lucky winner is picked every week. Hurry before the offer ends!

ABOUT THE AUTHOR

Dianne lives in Huntington Beach, California, with her husband, Tom, a former California State Senator, and her boxer dog, Kelly. Her passions are cooking, reading, and dogs, so whenever she has a little free time, you can either find her in the kitchen, playing with Kelly in the back yard, or curled up with the latest book she's reading. Her award winning books include:

Cedar Bay Cozy Mystery Series

Cedar Bay Cozy Mystery Series - Boxed Set

Liz Lucas Cozy Mystery Series

Liz Lucas Cozy Mystery Series - Boxed Set

High Desert Cozy Mystery Series

High Desert Cozy Mystery Series - Boxed Set

Northwest Cozy Mystery Series

Northwest Cozy Mystery Series - Boxed Set

Midwest Cozy Mystery Series

Midwest Cozy Mystery Series - Boxed Set

Cottonwood Springs Cozy Mysteries

Cottonwood Springs Cozy Mysteries - Boxed Set

Midlife Journey Series

Midlife Journey Series - Boxed Set

The Holly Lewis Mystery Series

Holly Lewis Mystery Series - Boxed Set

Miranda Riley Paranormal Cozy Mystery Series

A Cozy Cookbook Series

Coyote Series

Red Zero Series

Black Dot Series

Newsletter

If you would like to be notified of her latest releases please go to www.dianneharman.com and sign up for her newsletter.

Website: www.dianneharman.com,
Blog: www.dianneharman.com/blog
Email: dianne@dianneharman.com

PUBLISHING 3/10/20

THE WAR HERO'S WELCOME

BOOK 18

CEDAR BAY COZY MYSTERY SERIES

http://getbook.at/TWHW

Should be pretty straightforward

The war hero returns home

With his dog, Wicked

Both have been injured

But not everyone likes a war hero

Maybe Cash should have stayed in Afghanistan

At least there he knew who the enemy was.

When Kelly and Mike's son returns home from Afghanistan with a combat injury, all they want to do is help him recuperate. They never planned on becoming involved with kidnapping.

Good to have guard dogs when you need them.

This is the 18th book in the bestselling Cedar May Cozy Mystery Series by two-time USA Today Bestselling Author, Dianne Harman.

Open your smartphone, point and shoot at the QR code below. You will be taken to Amazon where you can pre-order 'The War Hero's Welcome'.

(Download the QR code app onto your smartphone from the iTunes or Google Play store in order to read the QR code below.)

Made in the USA
Las Vegas, NV
31 January 2021